CAMBRIDGE COMPANY

Since the publication of his first collection of stories, *East End at Your Feet* (1976), Farrukh Dhondy, prolific writer, playwright, scriptwriter and activist, has published several works of fiction, among them *Poona Company*, *Trip Trap*, *Bombay Duck*, *Black Swan* and the recent bestseller *Bikini Murders*; a biography of C.L.R. James; and a translation of the poetry of Jalaluddin Rumi.

During his stint as Commissioning Editor at Channel 4 TV from 1984 to 1987, he commissioned the works of Mira Nair, Deepa Mehta, Shekhar Kapur and Meera Syal. He has also scripted television serials for Channel 4 TV and the BBC in England and Star TV in India, and written screenplays for films such as *Bandit Queen*, *Split Wide Open*, *The Alexandria Quartet* and *Mangal Pandey: The Rising*.

Praise for *Cambridge Company*

'Written with nostalgia for those long-gone student days.'

– *Free Press Journal*

'A perfect compendium for those familiar with Farrukh Dhondy's *Poona Company* (1980). It continues the narrative...in a cold English university of the 60s. Multicultural, yes. Provocative, yes. Earthy, check. Lyrical, of course. This one is for Dhondy fans.'

– *OPEN*

'Episodic and vividly detailed, the memoir zips through scenes from university life...'

– *Hindustan Times*

CAMBRIDGE COMPANY

Farrukh Dhondy

hachette INDIA

First published in 2016 by Hachette India
(Registered name: Hachette Book Publishing India Pvt. Ltd)
An Hachette UK company
www.hachetteindia.com

This edition published in 2018

SRD

Hardback edition ISBN 978-93-5009-060-2
Paperback edition ISBN 978-93-5195-270-1
E-book edition ISBN 978-93-5195-133-9

Hachette Book Publishing India Pvt. Ltd
4th & 5th Floors, Corporate Centre,
Plot No. 94, Sector 44, Gurugram - 122003, India

Typeset in Californian FB 10.5/13.8
by InoSoft Systems, Noida

Printed and bound in India by
Manipal Technologies Limited, Manipal

CONTENTS

CONTENTS

SAY DRY SHERRY

I DIDN'T KNOW how one bought a ticket at Liverpool Street station; I fretted about it all the way on the Tube. Did they sell tickets months in advance like the Indian Railways? Would the queues last eight hours as they did at Bombay railway station? Was there a way of bribing the guard and getting on the train of one's choice? I expected there to be a rush – this was the first day of term and the undergraduates of Cambridge would be surely massing there. Perhaps I should have gone a day earlier. I felt embarrassed at being so non-street-wise.

I kept telling myself it would be okay. There'd be a queue like everywhere else and I'd left myself enough time. I lugged my suitcase up the escalator. I didn't know that the convention was to stand on the left so I took up the whole width of it, not understanding why the lady behind me was 'tch tching' her disapproval. Did she know I was going to the University and for some reason disapproved? I was wearing what the director of the Tata Endowment for the Higher Education of Indians had dressed me in – the Bombay tailor's version of what she called 'Oxford bags' – pleated dark grey trousers and a blue-flecked tweed jacket.

No, I didn't want a return ticket.

And yes, the train ran every half-hour at 6 and 36 past.

I'd spent a few hectic days in London living in a boarding house that had been booked through the frustrating mechanism of long-distance phone calls; catching sight of a TV screen for the first time in my life, with a group of ball-gowned black girls singing 'Baby baby, where did our love go?'; buying a shirt in Oxford Street and walking back to South Kensington to conserve the bus fare pennies; counting the tube stations as I passed them on foot, pretending to play the game of surprising myself with 'surface London' after having gone under it in the geometric illusion of the Tube.

By hectic days I don't mean parties or gatherings – I mean the alertness to accents I had never heard before; my embarrassment at having to ask the Scottish landlady to repeat her instruction to me ten times; the uncertain choice between saying 'beg your pardon' and the interrogative 'sorry'. I decided to adopt the latter immediately after my encounter with the young man in the Mod jacket I met at dinner.

After buying the ticket and locating the platform for the next train to Cambridge, I fell prey to a new anxiety. What would I do if a porter approached me and offered to carry my bag to the train, as they would on any Indian railway station?

I went through a brief debate in my mind. This was egalitarian England. I would neither need nor have servants here. Everyone I met in India, who knew I was off to Cambridge, mentioned this fact as if it were the most significant feature of Western civilization and modernity. 'You'll have to do everything for yourself, you know, shopping, cooking, washing up, cleaning, doing your bed...'

'Really? I thought I was going to carry a couple of Goan ayahs with me,' I responded, knowing the sarcasm would be lost. No servants was what I wanted, having come to the conclusion that they were not only a moral anachronism but also made more work for their employers who had to see through their dodges, deal with their knotted family disputes and problems, support their extended net of relatives through illnesses, etc. However, the guidebooks to life at Cambridge, which students at the University had published, said that each undergraduate would be assigned a servant, known traditionally as the 'bedder' or the 'gyp', who would clean my room and look after me in college. Socialism could wait. After all, the practice had been going on for hundreds of years and was not considered demeaning.

So what was one to do about the luggage porters? Should I openly espouse the egalitarian philosophy I was determined to adopt now that I had shaken the dust of caste- and class-ridden India off my shoes? Around me other young men also going 'up', as the guidebook and a reading of *Brideshead Revisited* had taught me to say, were dragging their own bags and sacks. Very few of them were dressed as I was, in my poor imitation Edwardian undergraduate garb with a modest tie and pin. They were wearing, for the most part, the narrow trousers of the mid-sixties and the long jackets of Mods or the leather and jeans gear of intellectual rockers; their luggage was rugged, battered and interesting with protruding cricket bats and tennis rackets. A few carried duffel bags stuffed with God knows what clobber from their public school sixth form 'prefects' studies'. I'd read about those.

No porters approached me. The train was crammed. I was longing to start up conversations with the other men in the carriage, who greeted each other, caught up on their doings in the vacations, or busily buried their heads in books, but I didn't know how. There may have been women but I didn't see them. It was going to be a male world.

The train stopped outside Bishop's Stortford. I told myself it would soon go again. This was Britain and trains run on time.

After fifteen minutes it was still there. The young man sitting opposite me slapped down his sports magazine and stormed down the corridor, made his investigations and returned with a look of contempt on his face.

'Signal stuck. The little man who pulls the rope must have gone for his tea or fallen asleep. Fucking Beeching.' I smiled in agreement. I didn't know whether Beeching was a place, a person or an activity.

'It better get going, I've got bloody socks to wash and dry,' he said and proceeded to take a sports bag down from the overhead rack and remove a wash load of dirty, muddy, thick cotton and woollen socks out of it, which he dumped in a heap, proceeded to pair and returned to the bag.

'Where do the missing ones go?' he asked me.

I tried 'sorry?' on him, not knowing what he meant.

'You wear socks where you come from, don't you?'

'Yes,' I said. One or two of the others looked over their papers to see who was engaged in this bizarre exchange. The sock man had blonde wavy hair and was wearing a huge coat.

'Missing. Separated. Divorced. The struggle of life is to keep pairs of socks together.'

I thought he was being chatty and I got what he meant. I smiled.

'But you wouldn't know, would you? You probably have only one pair.'

I didn't know how to take that. Was he still joking? Were socks important? Another fellow looked round his newspaper and said, 'Oh, do shut up, Fleming. Why don't they move this fucking train?'

I took the letter giving me what I began to fear would be my final instructions for joining the University out of the inner pocket of my jacket. I was guarding it as a man on a parachute jump guards the toggle that opens it. It was the only piece of paper that told me that I had been accepted at Pembroke College and should present myself before noon on that very day.

I had calculated on having an hour to spare even after making my way from the railway station to the town by bus or by shared cab as the donated, three years out-of-date, student guide, my other lifeline, told me to do. However, we were stuck outside Bishop's Stortford and the spare hour shrank to a quarter and then to ten and five minutes and disappeared in negative, nightmare figures. Then the train began to move. I was desperate.

The sock man got to the taxi queue at the same time as I did. I would have tried the bus if they'd have taken my suitcase, but it was noon when we got to Cambridge station and I decided to gamble part of my last two pounds, the only money I had, on a taxi. The next scholarship cheque for spending-money, precisely two pounds and fifteen shillings, would arrive in the post in three days. I'd hold out. Gandhi went on hunger strike for months. Sock man suggested we share and diligently took half the fare from me when I got off at Pembroke, the first stop.

I had never seen anything like it outside the picture books. Stone walls and enclosed courts. Gates like those of castles in the movies. There was a queue outside the Porters' Lodge and men I took to be the new intake were looking at notices on the boards which contained lists of names and allocation of rooms.

I fought my way to the lists. My heart sank. My name wasn't on them, but I didn't know whether it was supposed to be. My note had said I should present myself at the Porters' Lodge so I lined up with others who weren't looking at the noticeboards. Another anxiety assailed me. I didn't know whether to refer to the porters as 'sir' or not. I took my cue from the man in front of me who called the porter Harry and asked him to 'be a good fellow and...' I didn't understand the rest. I decided to call the porter nothing.

'And you are?'

I told him my name. He looked down his clipboard. *Please, God, let it be there.* It was. He found it and said, 'You are one of Mr Dewey's and he'll see you at 12.15 p.m. in his rooms today. And you are on V staircase in the new block. I'll get your keys.'

'But it's already one o'clock.'

'Then you're late,' he said.

'So what shall I do?'

'Go to your room and hope for the best.'

'What will Mr Dewey think?' I asked.

'Search me, young man. What can one ever say about what Mr Dewey will think or has thought or is thinking?' His declaration amused him. He looked around for approval.

'I've just come from London,' I said.

'Been there once, didn't like it,' he said and proceeded to fiddle with keys from his drawer.

'I've actually come from India, a few days ago,' I said, aware that this was turning into something of a Lewis Carroll exchange.

There must have been a note of pleading or panic in my voice, because he caught it and, handing over his clipboard to another porter, he stepped out from behind his flapped counter.

'Come on, I'll take you to your rooms, Mr India.'

I followed him dragging my one, neat bag.

'About Mr Dewey, my tutor...'

'He *was* your tutor. I don't know what view he'll take of these goings-on,' he said.

My heart sank to my black shoes. Would they send me back? It wasn't my fault. First appointment, first dereliction...

Harry the porter suddenly relented.

'Get a piece of paper and a pen. Write Mr Dewey a note and stick it in his pigeonhole in the senior common room. He'll get back to you. Don't get airiated young man.'

'How? I mean, I'm not airiated. (I knew it must mean something I shouldn't be.) I mean how will he get back to me?'

'Through your own pigeonhole in the junior common room,' he said, resigned by now to dealing with a complete novice or a foreign fool.

'And where is the senior common room?' This was reasonable.

'In Spencer quad,' he said, smiling. 'Look, come back after you've left your gear and I'll give you a book with a map of where you are, Mr Dhondy.'

Now he turned kind and chatty and asked about where I was from and left me at my door with my keys, telling me that I could buy writing paper from a shop down the street.

I got the paper. I fetched the map of the college that the Porters' Lodge kept for tourists and worked out where the respective common rooms were. I wrote that note again and again, tearing up the drafts, improving the shaky handwriting, trying to cut out the terror and apology from it, trying to get the tone right. My room was on the second floor, modern, bare, comfortable. I had never seen a central heating radiator before and I instantly burnt my right hand on it. My writing hand. It hurt, but I worked at the note.

My final draft was brilliant:

'Dear Mr Dewey,

I am afraid my train was late, but I have arrived and will contact you as soon as you want.'

I wrestled with 'want' and 'require' and with adding further excuses, but decided that that was all that was necessary. I found the senior common room which was largely deserted, went through the open door and put the note in the pigeonhole marked 'John Meredith Dewey. Dean'.

Every half-hour I went down to the junior common room to check if he had replied. It occurred to me that I could hang around Spencer quad and pretend to be appreciating the architecture until such time as a person who may or may not have been Mr Dewey emerged from the senior common room and went toward the junior one. Only, I'd put myself in the position of waiting for Godot – I didn't know what he looked like.

I decided I'd go back to my room and come down to check at ten-minute intervals. Should I unpack? Or would that be inviting fate? I experimented with the curtains, I tried the bed. I was hoping I'd sleep there that night. I was far away from home, if there was such a place. I was twenty years old.

On my fourth trip down I found the note. It was written on his own embossed letterhead.

'Dear Dhondy,

You may have arrived, but the verb "to contact" has not. I shall see you in my rooms at 5.10. Don't lose the way.

Meredith Dewey'

I put on my tweed jacket and tie, shone my shoes with a new hanky and, guided by the map, went looking for 'M' staircase. It was in what looked to me like a large red-brick house with gables and endless passages, out of character with the stone courts, parts of which I later learnt dated back to the thirteenth and fourteenth centuries. I found the imposing wooden stairway and climbed to the top landing with just one heavy oak door off it. A black painted patch with white writing on the wall at the bottom of the stairs declared that these were Mr Dewey's rooms, but there was nothing to confirm that I hadn't taken the wrong turning on the way in this monkey-house of a building. Was I in the right place? The door was slightly ajar and someone was playing the piano, competently or not, I was unqualified to judge. It was 5.09 and I knocked and waited. The playing continued.

I knocked again. I waited for thirty seconds between knocks, counting. I pulled out the note he'd left me to confirm the time and knocked again, louder and louder, till I was afraid of the sound myself.

I poked my head round the door.

'I'm Farrukh Dhondy,' I said.

A short, slightly balding man with merry eyes and mischief on his lips, with pink cheeks and eyebrows that went up and down very articulately, was playing the piano. He wore a dog collar.

'How very interesting,' he said, and carried on playing the piano, looking up from the keys only for a brief second. I froze halfway in the door, uncertain as to whether to retreat.

The game was over. He rose from his stool.

'You'd better come in, then,' he said.

I muttered something about being sorry that the train was late, but he waved the comment away. He picked up his very fragrant pipe and lit it.

'What will you drink?'

'Anything,' I said.

'Don't say "anything",' he protested as he went to the drinks cabinet, 'say dry sherry.'

'I'd like some dry sherry,' I said.

He handed me the glass, which he'd filled.

'Dhondy, you are a man of taste,' he said in sombre, low, mock-admiring tones.

We sipped the sherry.

'Have you been shown to your rooms? You're in the new block. It has central heating, so we put all the wogs there,' he said.

I had never heard or read the word before. He probably sensed that and explained.

'Indians and Africans, you know. Now we've got you and we've got Matty Kambona this year and there's the Vanier boy whom Dr King brought over last year from the Caribbean. So there's three of you and assorted Americans. Have you met any of them?'

'No one yet,' I said.

'You should put yourself about a bit,' he said and broke into an endearing smile.

Was it always to be like this? I had come to a temple where the priests were devotees of irony. It took me some time to learn that the confidence of the place was not in its traditions but in its self-mockery. I walked out into the quad. It was venerable, it was English and I had learnt that the two were incompatible, that one had to be proud but had to retain the right to jeer in case the gods got the impression that you were really taking yourself seriously.

DONKEY JACKETS

IN MY FIRST few days I got stuck with a crowd I would later be acquainted with but not as my University friends. They were men whom I first met at table in Hall, college mates who suggested we explore the town together. Then I made friends with my neighbour, Beresford 'Berry' Summers, who introduced himself as a Tory and a public school alumnus who hated what was happening to the Tory party since they'd elected that 'grammar school twerp, Ted Heath' to lead their party. He explained the difference between public and grammar schools as that of birth and jumped-up, specious accomplishment. I got to know that public schools were really private ones, a tiny paradox which had ceased to bother those who used the term. His distinctions struck me as snobbish but he was my neighbour and displayed no snobbery towards my not being British. He talked about Billy Bunter and the Indian maharaja in that tale. Perhaps he thought that an Indian who had got to Cambridge must be a maharaja.

He was in the room next to mine, overlooking the section of the college wall which was used, after the college gates shut each night, to import girlfriends and one-night stands. Berry kept a basket of soft rotten apples, all grown in his family garden, he said, to throw at them if the clatter of their coming or going over the bicycle sheds disturbed his envious dreams. 'Let's make them happy,' he would say.

I was often woken up by the sounds of his triumphant cries at having scored a hit and then the sound of irate lovers storming up the stairs to sort out the apple thrower. On several occasions the shouts turned to physical fights on the landing after doors were banged and accusations of cowardice issued. Berry had more artillery than the apples. He kept buckets of water, which he threw over challengers as they stormed up the stairs, making them even 'happier'. After once futilely offering the combatants some pacifist philosophy and protesting that I was trying to sleep, I stayed out of their way.

On my first morning after a restless, self-congratulatory and still scary night, I met my 'bedder', Mrs Baldwin, or Mrs B as she said she'd like to be called. She spoke with what Berry told me was a 'Fens accent'. He pronounced her acceptable.

I spent that first day trying to commit to memory the plan of the town, and under the tutelage of Berry, buying coffee and then mugs, a maroon kettle with a whistle, teaspoons and a cheap saucepan from Woolworths and trying to pretend that the routines of the college were second nature to me.

Then that night I couldn't find my pyjamas. I could have sworn I left them on the bed with the wet towel after my morning shower, before I went out. I looked in the wardrobe, in the drawers, in my now empty suitcase. They were nowhere. Could Mrs B have taken them by mistake? Stolen them? Surely she didn't need the pair of silk pyjamas given to me as a parting joke by friends in Poona!

I slept naked that night, feeling slightly salacious, never having slept naked in my crowded Indian household. I thought how I'd have to save up for weeks to buy new pyjamas, how the relationship with my 'bedder', to whom I couldn't mention the missing clothes, had been soured forever. In the middle of the night, restless with these concerns, I thrust my hands under the pillow. I felt silk. I felt a fool. I didn't know that this was a traditional resting place for what Berry, hearty, boat-rowing and rugger-playing, called 'jim-jams'.

In those first days there were other disasters to which I didn't confess. Of course the college didn't have a dhobi. One had to go to the basement of G staircase and use the washing machines and dryers that ran all day and most of the night. Imitating the men I had seen crossing the quadrangle, I took my bundle down. I had never seen a washing machine before. I looked for instructions and found a list of typed ones on the wall. It specified 'detergent' which I guessed was the soap powder that Berry had presciently made me buy. He had specifically said that the large box would be more economical as they were giving 140 per cent for the price of 100 per cent. Nothing on the box or the wall told me what quantity to use and there was no one at hand to ask. I had never washed clothes before.

A couple of sullen men came down the basement steps and took their washing away in plastic bags. I waited about for a friendly face but didn't encounter one, so I emptied the box of washing powder into the little sliding tray, slammed the door and followed the instructions for turning the dial. I kept pouring the powder into the machine through the open door. How else would it make contact with the clothes and the water? The typed instruction sheet jauntily said it would take almost an hour. I'd come back later.

I went about my business, identifying the colleges and making sure I knew where the lecture theatres were. I ventured back to G staircase that night and there was a cluster of four or five undergrads waiting at the top of the dank stairs.

'Don't go down there,' one said, 'some idiot has flooded the place.'

'But my clothes...' I started to say and then I spotted it. The foam was rising up the stone staircase. It was nearly through the basement doorway and into the quad.

I thought it best to leave and let matters settle, best to pretend that I didn't even know that that was the laundry room. I lived for hours in terror of discovery. I sneaked out late that night and went down the stairs. The bubbles had subsided and the foamy mess was now at about knee level. The machine had stopped pumping it out and the bubbles were drying naturally but taking their time. I pulled my clothes out and bundled them off, still wet, to the basin in my room. It took me hours in the little sink to get the soap out of them one by one. I went exhausted to lectures the next morning.

In those first few weeks I wrote airmail letters full of boasts and confidence to my parents, to my friends, to my aunts and mainly to my girl, Mala, to whom I'd promised undying affection and with whom I'd made the contradictory pact to part in mature and mutual freedom.

◆

I soon felt self-conscious in my tweed jacket and baggy trousers. No one else was wearing this ridiculous uniform.

In Poona I had grown a beard at sixteen, a tribute in part to the defiance of the beatniks Kerouac and Ginsberg about whom I'd read. I wore the cotton drainpipes and narrow-collared shirts that were, in imitation of some imagined American rock fashion, à la mode in my little town on the Deccan plateau of western India.

Of course I had no idea about the sartorial exactitudes of the Mods or the Rockers. It would have been absurd to try and adopt the style of either. I saw them as part of the infantile carnival of Britain which I couldn't join. But I had to get rid of the scholarship tweeds. I had to save up the money and find a direction. And only one forcefully suggested itself.

A college is a small community and you get talking to people in queues and common rooms, in Hall and in the crowded bars of the closest pubs. I was getting a measure of the place; apart from Berry, my first friend and guide, there lived at the bottom of my staircase a heavy Irishman fresher who was reading English. Paul Danaher came from what he called a working-class family and had won a scholarship to Dulwich College in South London. Over the bottle of duty-free whisky which I had brought into England and kept like a miser for weeks, he told me that his school had been founded by James Alleyn, a Shakespearean actor of some long-gone century who saw ghosts and wanted to reconcile himself to God through good works. One of the results of these works was Paul.

He knitted sweaters in his spare time – for himself, for his relatives and eventually a long grey one for me. He was blue-eyed and large, with shoulder and back muscles big enough to give the impression of a crouched, if not hunched, back. It wasn't a deformity. It was the self-effacement of his stance: his feet together, like those of a trained choir boy and his hands clasped high across his chest, his whole demeanour apologetic for his existence, yet he would argue and persist, through the night if necessary. His most passionate arguments were about the workers of Britain and the upper classes who went to public schools and then came on to Oxford and Cambridge and perpetuated the iniquitous divisions of a social system which had to be put to the sword. He told me he was the scholarship boy at the public school and he had a mission to abolish the system that afforded him charitable emancipation on the grounds that he was smarter than the rest of the boys he played with.

I met this passion again and again in new friends, over cups of coffee in the rooms of different men, and found that under the corporate idea of the college to which I, with ideas gleaned from books, so much subscribed, there was a current of hatred. There were those who had come to Cambridge to join the system in order ultimately, in their working and political lives, to destroy it.

Paul used to wear, apart from his hand-knitted sweaters, a navy jacket which seemed to me to be made out of a thick discarded blanket. It was the uniform of several people whose defiance struck a chord in me and I enquired about this garment and was told it was the uniform of the working class. D.H. Lawrence's father might have worn one. I determined to get myself one of these 'donkey jackets'. I saved the pounds, skimping on the half pints of beer, the textbooks, cancelling the daily order of a half pint of milk and drinking my coffee black and eking out the toothpaste and soap. Finally I had saved the price of one and went out to buy it.

The man in the shop made me try several and assured me that the one he was inducing me to choose was the right one. It was grey and had a fur collar which he said would keep me warm. I couldn't explain to him that it was the symbolism I was after, not the practicality. I didn't want to be warm. I wanted to get rid of my silly jacket which Mrs Vesugarh, the scholarship director back in Bombay, thought stood for something she valued, whereas I had found that it only stood for the fact that I stood out as someone who was out of touch and slightly pathetic. I went proudly back to college to show my new jacket to Paul who knew I'd been saving up.

His face fell. I asked him to be frank.

'That's not the real McCoy,' he said, 'It's okay, it'll keep you warm, but it's a travelling salesman's jacket.' He began to laugh.

I took the jacket back and changed it for the rough black

one which was cheaper so the man had to give me some money back. I was grateful for this and took Paul for a drink. He told me the virtues of the different ales and I learnt how one bought 'rounds'.

Apart from Paul, there was another man who made his mark on me, captivating my attention from the moment I first heard him boasting in Hall. He was sitting opposite me and for a moment I wondered if one of the lecturers, the dons, had somehow got misplaced and ended up eating on the undergraduate benches. He assumed that everyone would know who he was and that everyone wanted to talk to him and in that he set himself apart from the Brits. And then his accent. I didn't know it was Australian. I had never met an Australian before but the Americans who had introduced themselves to me, Yale scholars called Sandy Mack and Stephen Greenblatt, seemed interested in its vowel sounds and engaged him that first day in Hall in a conversation about accents.

This older man with the ability to quip about everything from the college architecture, the portraits of the English martyrs in Hall and the remarks of F.R. Leavis at a tutorial he'd attended, to the potatoes we were served, had deep-set eyes and a constant disturbed blink. At dinner he was the entertainment and I went back day after day and sought him out in order to listen to his sour clips and comments. They seemed loaded with instant wisdom, with a way of looking that was clear, witty and idiosyncratic.

He was in our year. He too had just come, though his patter had nothing of the stranger in it. He had already made Cambridge and its ethos part of his life and plan. He had some special dispensation to live outside the college, but seemed to know its history in aggressive detail and was very interested in the fact that the room atop N staircase, known in college as the Crow's Nest, had been occupied, not so many years previously, by Ted

Hughes. I knew who Ted Hughes was. I had even bought, in Bombay, a slim volume of his poems in which he was paired with Thom Gunn. The Australian, it seemed to me, knew everything and could turn his mind to any topic under the sun that was mentioned at table. And what struck me in the first week was that he gathered no disciples. He would accept an invitation to have a coffee after dinner, but while the rest of the gathering was halfway through their Maxwell House, Clive James would hurry away. He had an appointment; he had things to write.

Later that term he approached me and asked me to read in a Poetry of the Thirties occasion he was organizing. I said I'd do it and went along to the meeting he'd called in some don's rooms. He had several copies of an anthology which he handed to each of the readers he had chosen, bookmarked at the poems they were to read. He went through a brief rehearsal with each of us. I was to read several poems of C. Day Lewis. I took away the book and made sure that I knew the English pronunciation of all the words.

I read the C. Day Lewis to the audience in the Old Library. There was sherry after. I was proud of having being chosen to read poems to a public, paying audience in my first term. Berry, my neighbour, who was hardly a poetry man, attended out of loyalty and out of a sense that he had to keep an eye on me and stop people taking advantage. Afterwards he said it was good and said that people had remarked that Clive James had chosen the readers well, because my Indian accent was a good substitute for the Welsh one he couldn't find amongst the college literati.

LAWRENTIAN LOVE

THE TEST OF strength of my first love came by airmail letter. Mala casually mentioned that she was dating a fellow named Darius. I knew this fellow vaguely. She wrote about being together with him and seeing films or going for picnics or to dances at the army clubs where she was, being the commandant's daughter, treated like a princess.

The letters and the mention of this rich boy made a knot in my stomach. She would sign the letters with a kiss and at first there were two letters a week, but then they dwindled to one and then one every two or three weeks. I wrote to her twice a week and committed myself to that pattern. I would describe the things I'd done, the day-to-day things like going to a pub and what one did there – ordering at the bar and paying for the drink when it came.

I didn't tell her about Enid. I felt guilty and justified at the same time. We had a tryst – separated by thousands of miles and possibly for three years, we would go our own ways in our friendships, in our allegiances and in our potential romances. The notion was born of the ideas we had picked up from reading Sartre, Camus, D.H. Lawrence and Henry Miller. We told ourselves in all the wisdom of our teenage years that we had a tryst with freedom. That if the love between us was strong enough it would only be tested and never replaced by infidelities which we were in the following years bound to, and therefore free to, have.

I had no idea when we parted that Mala believed in this tryst or in the notions of freedom and attachment behind it. She followed perhaps where I led. I had never considered how either of us would communicate the truth of any infidelity even though our intellectual ramblings sought to banish the notion of 'infidelity'. Mala had taken to reading the writers I mention because I gave her the books and we discussed them as she read. I knew that she believed that these readings, and the pretentious discussions we would have in our 'gang' about the abstracts that arose from them, put her on a plane of intellectual achievement above the girlfriends she knew from school.

'I know where you get stupid ideas from,' her mother and her mother's husband, whom she refused to address as stepfather, would say. Mala called her mother's husband 'Tutu', which was the pet name her mother and the other officers of the army in which he'd made his earlier career used for him.

And though the nagging feeling of being unfaithful stayed firmly in the back of my mind and settled itself in the bottom of my spine, I knew I was excited by the possibility of sex and even the discovery of some subtle definition of love with Enid.

I was bewildered to learn that Enid drew her ideas about love and fidelity and the tussle of love between male and female from the very same sources – from D.H. Lawrence, Henry Miller, Lawrence Durrell, Albert Camus and other fashionable writers at the time. Enid would, as Mala had learnt to do, quote them.The only other Enid I had heard of was the children's writer whose books all Indian children educated in English were introduced to. Enid Imelda Schneider admitted that her first name had been chosen by her English mother who was, even as an adult, a great fan of Blyton. She didn't like the name but didn't want to be called Imelda or any shortening of that name either.

'I am stuck with it,' she said when she first introduced herself at an audition I was holding at the Pembroke Players. The college society had chosen me as one of its three 'nursery production' directors after I had submitted my sketch of the absurdist plays I wanted to stage.

Though I was reading Natural Sciences, with an intention to specialize in Physics, with which I had graduated in Poona, in the first few weeks at Cambridge I was attracted, out of my natural inclinations, to enrol in the literary and dramatic societies which would have me. The Pembroke Players seemed a good place to start.

Enid auditioned for a part I had already made up my mind to gift to another, in my mind, more energetic actress. That was fortunate as Enid landed the lead role in a parallel nursery production so when we set up a friendship which turned into a relationship, I couldn't be accused of casting-couch favouritism.

'I wasn't pretty enough?' she asked, when I told her she hadn't got the part.

'On the contrary. Your features are too refined for an absurdist play. I chose an actress with features that can contort like a rubber mask.'

Flattery got me her attention and we decided to have a drink that evening. We discussed D.H. Lawrence and the myth and mystery of sexual interaction. She had read all the relevant novels and stories and we talked with an intensity which barely concealed the desire on both our parts to subject the Lawrentian ethic to practical experiment.

Enid told me she had a boyfriend in London and I told her about Mala. I left her at the entrance to her college after the pub and we agreed to meet after lectures the next day at the Sedgwick

Buttery, the student café on the site of the University's Arts faculty.

I cycled there after maths lectures. She said I needn't rush off after rehearsals, which we both had to go to at six, to dine in Hall that evening; the women's colleges had pantries and cooking facilities on every staircase and she had bought the ingredients to make spaghetti with some recipe she had picked up on a holiday in Italy. I should catch up with her after rehearsals and we could go to her room instead.

She made dinner as I sat in the kitchen and talked to her. She had bought a bottle of wine which we shared over dinner and finished it off sitting in her room.

Guests had to be out of her college by ten o'clock. Similar strictures applied in the men's colleges, except that there a 'bedder' came in in the mornings to tidy the rooms and do the beds. They would, of course, discover any guests who had broken regulations and stayed the night. The trespass would be reported and the student and perhaps the guest, if he or she were a member of the University, would face admonition and punishment.

Every college, though, had a night path in and out, avoiding the Porters' Lodge and everyone – undergraduates, dons and the porters policing the rules – knew these exits and entrances. My tutor, very early on, asked me if I knew the way in and out after hours over the bicycle shed and down the lamp post in Tennis Court Road. I said it had been pointed out to me.

The women's colleges didn't employ bedders. Female students were expected to tidy their own rooms and do their own beds. This meant that there would be no immediate supervision of the women's rooms in the morning and a man who had stayed overnight would have to remain till a respectable hour of the day, when he could plausibly have come in, to go out again.

That night we each steered the conversation round to

D.H. Lawrence, to what he really intended to say in *Lady Chatterley's Lover* and how instinctual understanding was key to the sexual content of some of his short stories.

It was verbal foreplay and both Enid and I knew it and acknowledged it when we talked in lower and lower tones, putting our faces closer and closer together till we kissed.

'Let's try sex without love,' Enid said.

'Can one really separate them?' I asked, knowing it was a negative rhetorical question. Of course I could, but could she?

My only sexual encounters had been with Mala.

'You haven't done this very often, have you?' Enid asked, as she took her trousers down, to reveal stockings fastened to her knickers. I was spellbound, my heart pounding as she took them off to reveal the blonde pubic hair on to which she placed my hand, grasping it in hers.

Her hair wasn't soft, but grassy and thick. She smiled at me because she knew I was trembling.

'So no Lawrentian confidence, then,' she said.

I had to stop myself, stop my pounding heart. I gently removed my hand from her crotch and got undressed as she took her top off and sitting on her bed, asked me to unhook her bra.

I did. She had firm round breasts with pink nipples; she pulled me on to her as she lay back on her single bed. We kissed passionately with our tongues in each other's mouths and biting each other's lips.

Enid got up and bolted the door and went to a drawer from which, from under her underwear, she pulled out a plastic box and a tube of paste.

I hadn't seen a diaphragm before. She took the rubber disc out of its case and applied the spermicide from the tube to it. Then bending her knees she tucked it inside her.

'Much better than condoms,' she said.

We made love till dawn and the light crept in through the curtains. She warned me against making the least noise. The girls on either side wouldn't like it or tolerate it because even though she knew that several of the girls on her staircase had men round, they probably hadn't stayed the night.

In the morning she didn't go down to breakfast. She said we should stay in her room till the other girls in the corridor had gone. Then we could go downstairs and out into one of the other quads and return and be seen going up to her room.

We spent the day together walking along the Cam on the Backs.

'Without love, remember?' she said. 'We don't want to fall for each other. It'll be much too inconvenient and we have a lot to do.'

'Do you mean we shouldn't pair off and can have other, how shall I put it, adventures?'

'No, not quite that. But you've told me you've got Mala and I told you I've got this bloke...'

'Who is this bloke, what's his name, for God's sake. You talk about your encounters, but haven't given me any indication of who the hell or how old he is or what he does. What's the secret?'

'It's no secret now. It was for a year. His name is Conrad and he's a teacher, a schoolteacher.'

'In your old school?'

'Yes!'

'Let me guess, he taught you English.'

'Yes!'

'And his favourite writer – no, his obsession, was D.H. Lawrence?'

'Yes!'

'And this was a kind of Lawrentian detached and observed but intense experience which you will report to him in London?'

I must have turned away from her, because she put her hand on my shoulder and gently pulled me towards her.

'No, it wasn't and I won't. I am just going to try hard not to fall for you,' she said and kissed me, holding me tight.

I kissed her back and then I heard a shout behind me.

'Oi! Frook, Frook, Frook!'

I turned round. Hyder, one of the Pakistani students I knew, was looking across the river at us carrying a sack of books.

'*Tujhe mil gaya yaar, mujhey bhi dilaa de*!'

'Who's that, what's he saying?' Enid asked.

'He's called Hyder. Pakistani. He says "You got some, now get me some too!"'

'Oi, get your own!' Enid shouted. 'Though with a face and mentality like that you'll have a hard day's night.'

'What the hell is she saying?' Hyder asked in Urdu.

'She says the girls are all this side of the river, so you'd better learn to swim.'

'Eh, don't be silly, yaar, Frook!' He shouted even as Enid led me away.

TALCUM

I SUPPOSE I must have known about Christmas vacations, but until they crept up on me, I had not realized that the natives would go home, the colleges would be deserted and dark and a handful of Indians and Pakistanis would survive the winter in friendly nationalistic groups at hostels and boarding houses.

I had realized in that first term that there were some rich Indians about, sons of industrialists and of course Rajiv Gandhi, grandson of Jawaharlal Nehru, whose mother Indira Gandhi was a minister and heiress-apparent to the prime ministership. But where were these Indians to be found? I once thought I saw a couple on the street, but how was I to approach first? They might have been second and third years, well settled and hostile to the approaches of freshmen straight from the unfashionable societies of India.

So it was with a feeling of gratitude that, a few weeks into first term, I received an invitation in my pigeonhole from one P.D. Gupta at Trinity. The invitation said I was to go for drinks in his rooms as he had invited all the first year Indians he could find. I admired his diligence and his research.

He lived in Whewell Court across the street from the main college. Unlike my room which was airy and new and centrally heated, this room had the real atmosphere of being in the ancient stone precincts of monastic Cambridge. Ten or fifteen young men were crammed into his two rooms. He dispensed sherry. I asked him which year he was in and he said he too had just come. His air of having been there for decades was a fraud. He was from Calcutta and seemed to think that bestowed some kind of distinction on him.

I tried to memorize the names of the Indians who had gathered there, my fellow invitees. Two in particular were to become good friends. These were Darryl D'Monte, and Michael Mascarenhas, a young man in a blazer and a Fitzwilliam Hall badge and scarf. I had a Pembroke scarf but found out very early that it was much too collegiate and hearty and undergraduate-like to wear it voluntarily. One had to disown all marks of belonging in order to belong.

The subject turned to politics and it soon became evident that everyone in the room was pro-America in the Vietnam War and was of the opinion that the communists had to be restrained or they would make an assault on India next. I had never met this opinion before except in the pages of the *Reader's Digest*, a publication which I treated as lowbrow pap – the magazine my aunts ordered – even though I had over the years taken to sneaking a read of a little regular item called 'How to Increase Your Word Power' which listed obscure words and quizzed you with multiple choice answers as to their meaning.

I wasn't going to let the arguments pass. The US was imperialist. It had no business sending armies or planes or bombs or defoliating agents outside its borders. Cuba was perfectly within its rights and heroic for giving JFK a bloody nose over the Bay of Pigs. There was more danger from the debilitating influences of American culture and the exploitative tentacles of American capital invading us than there was of any external communists infiltrating or undermining India. I was in a minority of one. I was even asked with an upturned and pitying nose if I was a card carrier. I said I wasn't, I just hadn't been brainwashed by *Time* magazine, implying that the rest of them had. I had to tolerate the jeers that evening and felt shattered as I left. I was not going to become a political convert and if this was the sort of Indian who had come up to Cambridge with me, then I was in for severely isolating times.

In three terms, most of the Indian undergraduates in my batch, including Darryl, who was reading Economics at St Catherine's, and Michael, had been converted by their Economics lecturers and by the anti-American ethos of Liberal and Labour Britain in Oxbridge, to turn leftish and even virulently Marxist. By the second and third years there wasn't one of them who would not profess to be the most dedicated of Bolsheviks or Maoist disciples of the University's Sinophile professor of Economics, Joan Robinson, who even dressed in Chinese clothes and occasionally in a conical hat.

I looked out for Rajiv Gandhi. He had his own entourage, friends of his from his schooldays in Doon, a posh school in the Himalayan foothills. I came across him once or twice, but he and his Indian set didn't mix with Darryl and the rest of our Indian set. The Rajiv gang had relatives or contacts in London and routinely enjoyed the patronage of the Indian High Commission and it was said that Rajiv and some of his mates owned fast cars, had their own flats and spent most of their time away from the campus. In his second year, my first, he failed his exams and was sent down. I don't suppose it mattered to him. He got a pilot's licence and became first a commercial pilot and then, years later, the prime minister of India.

At the same time and in my year there was a lout called Taher Ayub. He was the son of Ayub Khan, the military dictator of

Pakistan. He had large rooms, very near those of E.M. Forster in King's, and a large, cowed and sycophantic following of Pakistani undergraduates who paid court. They had bottles of spirits in their rooms, as though it was an army hospitality suite, and they had money which they spent on meals out each evening.

Taher wanted to cultivate some Indians to argue with them and subvert them. I was invited together with Darryl, who, by this time, was a firm friend. Out of curiosity, we went along to the Pakistani 'court' of the president's son.

The fellow was in his loose Pathan pyjamas, lounging on the sofa, scratching his crotch and aggressively demanding that the fawning crowd see to his comforts and those of his guests.

'*Dekhte nahin? Mehman aye hain?*' he shouted at a fellow called Chishti. '*Whisky lagao!*'

Chishti, his friend and fellow Pakistani undergraduate, jumped to it. There were others who hastened to get the ice out of the fridge and put the crisps they had shopped for on plates.

We were entertained and then subjected to an illiterate harangue on Kashmir to which we had decided in anticipation to make no reply and to smile and smile. Taher Ayub, raising his eyebrows in excited abuse, was joined by some of the others. He took our silence for being nonplussed by the cogency and ferocity of his argument. Chishti and one or two of the others knew that we were 'taking the piss' – an expression I had picked up in that first term.

Some of the Pakistanis, those without rich relatives in Britain, remained behind that first Christmas. They lived in a hostel in one of the leafier roads a short cycle ride away, if one cared to brave it in the snow. It was my first sight of the stuff. Term ended. The population of Hall had fallen to a trickle so that there was just one sitting. On the last day there were only four or five of us. However, each day the dons would come in from their common room, enter stage right, and settle down without a glance in the direction of the lower orders. From the walls the portraits of Cranmer and Ridley looked down, fellows who had been burnt at the stake for their views.

The autumn leaves had been swept away by a landscape vacuum cleaner and there was now a smell of fresh smoke in the air. Paul Danaher's gift of the long sweater that reached almost to my knees was making more and more sense as the cold set in. My aunts had knitted two turtleneck sweaters, one black, one green, from thick Kashmiri wool. Paul Danaher fingered them and envied the quality of the wool, marvelled at the patterns. The hobby had turned into a serious occupation.

Parents in estate cars came to pick their kids up. I helped Berry with his cases packed with sports equipment down the stairs to his parents' car.

The college was desolate in a day. I walked through the courts of the other colleges and there was the same silence. The porter stopped me as I returned.

'We shall be requiring your room from tomorrow, sir,' he said. 'You can move into digs, sir. I have a list of landladies that Mr Dewey said might serve you over Christmas.'

'What are the others doing?' I asked.

'There are no others,' he said, 'you're the last one. The rooms have to be made ready for the foreigners. Conferences.'

I knocked on several doors. Some of the addresses that the college porter gave me said that the room 'had been taken'. None of them was willing to say that they didn't want me to occupy it. I did, however, eventually find a cheap room at the top of a house in Fitzwilliam Street. It had a gas stove in the fireplace. The landlady pointed it out and said I could put my kettle on there if I was making tea. I had to put money in the gas meter. She said she didn't want any electric kettles about as there was no electric meter and she was paying the bills. She said she'd pulled the fuse out of the one electric socket capable of taking one so I needn't try and sneak an electric kettle past her. I said I couldn't afford an electric kettle at any rate.

I took the room and moved my few possessions into it. I had to make some careful economic calculations. The donkey jacket had cost me too much. I had to buy books from the weekly allowance and there had been no calculation in my scholarship trickle, paid in fixed instalments by the Tata London offices at 18 Grosvenor Place, W 1, for any Christmas lodging or boarding. It would have to come out of my allowance and amounted to almost all of it.

I had to last out two weeks, the length of time the college would close its doors to me. I had a saucepan and frying pan, potatoes and scrambled eggs, a bottle of oil, rice, the spices which were still packed in plastic bags inserted into sealed jars which my aunts had given me to carry from India, 'just in case', and some cans of pilchards and onions with which to curry them. The budget was tight but survival feasible. I could, I calculated, afford some cabbage and coffee and milk if I was careful. It wasn't miserable. Counting the pennies, stretching them, lasting out – it was living the bohemian life that writers whom I admired, Henry Miller or Lawrence Durrell, had lived. It made me feel a little closer to the George Orwell of *Down and Out* or the Knut Hamsun of *Hunger*.

Cambridge became a ghost town at Christmas. I wandered through the quads of the colleges and they were dark. Not a soul about. The Fens, the flatland around the town, got cold and windy and gave off a faintly watery smell. I went a couple of times to the last quadrangle of my college where my room was and wandered up. The key opened the door. It had been stripped and there was a strong smell of wood polish and wax which had been scrubbed into the parquet flooring. My nameplate was still at the bottom of the staircase, not painted on the wall, as were the names of the dons, but on a wooden plaque, which could be slotted out of a frame, to be replaced by that of the next occupant.

This old quad of the college was divided into two lawns – a small one enclosed on three sides by staircases, on which in the summer the college would play croquet, and the large grassy one lined with trees and landscaped to dip upwards towards the shrubbery and flowered plot which was Meredith Dewey's garden. On this big lawn some dons and select undergraduates would play boules, rolling the leather discs which looked to me like large rolls of measuring tape that surveyors would use or some obscure maritime instrument.

Dewey would potter around in his garden in his wellies, smoking his pipe, grubbing and rooting and nurturing the plants of whose provenance he was very proud. He'd call out from amongst the shrubs as I was passing.

'Look at this very fine thing. From India, foothills of the Himalayas.'

He pronounced Himalayas as it should be, with the accent on the second syllable, and not in the English way to rhyme with 'primmer players'. He was a zoologist by trade, but had meddled, as he put it, in old-fashioned botany.

Zoologist, botanist, physicist, historian, economist – one could understand how the descriptions used as a matter of fact by everyone at the University might apply to dons and those who had worked for years or accomplished something in these fields, but it came as something of an annoyance to hear these epithets applied by first-year undergraduates to themselves. 'I am a historian,' someone would say in introduction and Dewey referred to me as a 'scientist'. It was a humbling conceit. I was used to the thought that Newton and Rutherford were scientists and the likes of me would perhaps, after years, be worthy of taking a cloth to their shoes. But Cambridge had the assumption in its argot of distinction and success. Everyone, boys of nineteen and twenty, was someone and afforded this premature labelling.

Even if I didn't want to be called 'scientist', it was refreshing to be treated as a scholar and gentleman and as a grown-up. It also engendered a feeling of precariousness, that one day someone would catch on, the game would be up, the subterfuge exposed and the poseurs revealed, not as scientists and historians at all, but as frustrated and ruined boys. But perhaps by that time they would be scientists, economists, historians and the rest.

The empty college spooked me. It had a sense of uncaring, hollow permanence. It wasn't Cambridge; the fellowship was Cambridge. I remembered what Disraeli had said and someone, possibly a tutor, had repeated so that I memorized it: 'a university should be a place of light, of liberty and learning.'

So many times in the past term I had reminded myself that I had escaped. The Poona in which I grew up was a small town which hadn't been invaded by the industrial bustle of Bombay. My father's military career transferred him from one army station to another and there was as such no family home. I pictured myself at some Indian campus doing a postgraduate course, or perhaps preparing for the exams that would get me into the Indian Administrative or Foreign Services. I remembered the sinking feeling I used to get, cycling alone at dusk on the outskirts of the town, listening to the cackle of crows coming to rest in the banyan trees. It was for me the melancholy of the Indian twilight, a dread of the uncharted future and I determined even then to escape it.

Walking or cycling down the Cambridge streets that Christmas, I realized that there was no liberty, no learning and only a few hours of light. I was too cold and possibly too hungry to wake up with the sun so I stayed in bed each morning and got very little of the fast disappearing days. It was too cold to study and the sudden if temporary lack of money was confining.

On Christmas Eve and Christmas Day itself the fellows at the Pakistani hostel had each made plans to leave town. Having borrowed it from the college library and neglected to give it back on the date marked for its return, I started to read *War and Peace* for the first time. I knew the plot and had on occasion discussed the book, pretending to have read it so now I thought there was the opportunity to catch up on the pretence. I would sit under the blankets in the attic room in Fitzwilliam Street and get drawn into the Russian world of its characters, struggling to remember the different diminutives and titles by which each of them was called.

It was absorbing. Too absorbing. I had got to the battle of Borodino and the canons were exploding all around about me when I smelt metal burning. It wasn't the realistic invocation of Tolstoy but the three boiling potatoes which I had forgotten on the gas ring by the fire, my cooking facility. There was just a sticky burnt mess at the bottom of the pan and when I put it under the tap, the metal alloy gave way and the pan started to leak. Even if I could scrape the black mess out of it, it was no good. That was dinner ruined. I had a few cans of pilchards and the like but nothing else. I'd have to heat them on the ring and then save the cans to boil eggs in. My maroon gas kettle had a whistling mouth through which one filled and poured the water, but it wouldn't take eggs. I felt disgusted with myself, wretchedly stupid for having allowed it to happen.

In that mood I dressed, put on my turtleneck sweater and donkey jacket and walked down into the street. I'd walk this frustration off. There was no one on the streets. No traffic, no bikes. It was as though a nuclear bomb had exploded in the centre of civilization and I was the last survivor. Only as I walked into the town centre were there a few people hurrying by in the snow.

Under no other circumstances or inducements would I have entered the doors of Great St Mary's opposite King's and backing on the Town Square. It was the only building alive with light coming from its wooden doors. People were going in for the evening service. I didn't have to think about it. That's where I was going too.

The congregation was singing hymns as I entered. I had had something of an Anglican upbringing in Bishop's School, Poona, where I was sent from the age of eight to when I finished school at fifteen. I knew the hymns, though some of them seemed to have been put to different tunes. I knew the Lord's Prayer and I was used to Bible readings by a school prefect at the prayer assembly each morning. I could quote the overused passages – 'Yea, though I walk in the shadow of the valley of death...' or 'When I was a child, I thought as a child...' off by heart.

The congregation was standing to sing 'As pants the hart for cooling streams...' I stood next to a man who hadn't taken his coat off because the church was freezing. He offered to share his hymn book with me and I accepted for the fellowship, even though the words came automatically to me. Now, in England, singing in this congregation, I realized something about these words which had always eluded me in Poona, singing together with four hundred boys in white shorts and shirts with maroon-and-yellow-striped ties, most of them defiantly ragged. That the word 'hart' was not a misspelling by an Indian printer but meant what it said. It was a simile about longing for God being like the thirst of a pursued and panting deer. It fell into place. I had never made sense of 'As pants the hart' always wondering how 'pants' had intruded themselves into a hymn, though there seemed to be an obscure logic about this underwear getting sweaty and 'heated in the chase'.

Now clarity dawned and I sang louder: the thirsty, hunted deer looking for water; the hungry, lonely undergraduate, contenting himself with the fact that there was still a can of pilchards waiting in his room.

We sang three hymns or carols together and heard the preacher out and then the service was over. It was snowing as the congregation shuffled out and turned into Market Square or on to King's Parade. I hadn't looked at the man who had been sitting next to me. He was tall and had to lower his arm to share his book with me. But now I felt his presence behind me as he came up.

'Nice service,' he said.

'Yes, cheerful,' I agreed as we walked.

'Cold,' he said, 'and you have no gloves. Here, wear mine.'

'Oh no, no, no,' I said. 'I don't need gloves, never wear them, I've got pockets.'

'They are warm, those donkey jackets,' he said.

We were now fifty yards down. I supposed I was heading back to the room because there was nowhere else to go. I slipped on the snow which was coming down quite furiously and he grabbed me reflexively by the forearm and stopped me falling over.

We paused. I was grateful and for the first time I looked at his face. It was a big square face, reddish brown. He wore his hair in a centre parting, flopping on both sides of his forehead.

'I'm Harry,' he said and held out the hand he had removed the glove from.

I introduced myself. It was now clear that I couldn't object to his talking to me and walking alongside; he had just saved me from a stumble.

'You must be a student at the University?'

'I am,' I said. I had already tried slowing down my pace and quickening it, but he kept perfectly abreast of me.

'So you must live in town?'

I said, 'I have temporary digs, I normally live in college.'

'Ah, I live in King's Lynn,' he said and when I gave no sign of knowing where that was or being interested in his address he said it was fifty miles to the north and that he only came down to Cambridge for the church service and now he'd have to journey back by train. But he had time. Yes, he had time till the next train. A lot of time. Such a pretty place and he always felt so peaceful here, so gentle. I thought it an odd expression but strolled on determinedly through the cold.

'Well, yes,' I said. 'I've got to go back to my room and work.'

I turned down Fitzwilliam Street feeling slightly guilty for wanting to shake him off. He was harmless enough. He had needlessly but generously shared his hymn book and had grabbed me when I slipped.

'You are going into the warm,' he shouted after me. 'Will you be at the church service tomorrow?'

'I don't think so,' I said and could see that he was pleading to be invited to my room for a coffee.

'It may be four hours to my train, they cut the services at Christmas,' he said. His remark made me think of the panic I had felt when my first train to Cambridge was stuck on the tracks.

'You can come up for a few minutes and have a coffee,' I said. I wasn't looking forward to this. This wasn't the sort of company that would take the place of *War and Peace*.

He didn't remark on the stairs or the room. There was always the noise of television emanating from the basement where the landlady lived but on this day it was replaced by the sound of a man laughing and singing. The landlady had said that her son would be visiting at Christmas and that he would be occupying the bedroom on the first floor and I was not to wake her up thinking there were intruders. The rooms on the other floors were let to undergrads during term, but now they'd gone away and I was the lone tenant of the house and confined to the small attic room.

I let Harry follow me up the stairs and put the kettle on to boil. I had brought two mugs with me, anticipating company, and I made the coffee. We talked about the relative merits of different instant coffees and he told me about the supermarkets having their own house brands. 'They are the same coffee, the same goods. They get them from Nescafe or Maxwell House and put them in their own jars with their own labels and because they buy in bulk, they can sell cheaper.' He was proud of passing this information on and made sure that I understood the import of it. I could save on coffee by buying the house brands. I thanked him for the information.

As we spoke the gas fire died. The gas meter had to be fed. I dug in my pocket for my last coins. I had a shilling and put it in.

'I will feed the beast,' the fellow declared and came up with a handful of shillings and crowns. Before I could protest he knelt by the meter and fed them in one by one.

'No, no, you mustn't,' I protested.

'I'd love to keep my new friend warm,' he said.

I didn't know why, but the remark and his smirk made me feel uncomfortable. Of course I appreciated the gas meter being full of coins, but this was somehow wrong – taking money from a stranger.

Then, standing up as the kettle was on its way to whistling, he moved on to looking at my sparse shelves. He read out the labels on the jars. 'Ah Horlicks,' he said. 'Now if you drink Horlicks, try the house brands of TESCO or Sainsbury. But they can't say they are Horlicks and have to call themselves malted milk. But same thing and cheaper.'

It was probably useful advice but I wanted to be rid of him.

'I had better get back to work,' I said. That last word 'work' was something I had first heard in the context of study only in Britain. In India work was work, activity which paid the bills; solving maths problems or reading books was study.

I had lit the fire and he had taken off his coat. I was willing him to put it on and go and feeling ungrateful for the wish. I wanted to get back to the end of the battle of Borodino. But he showed no signs. I hastily poured the coffee, which he drank very slowly.

'I suppose you sleep on that bed,' said Harry and a weariness crept into his voice, as though to say he had seen a million such single beds and remarked to a million boys that they slept alone. Suddenly I realized what the game was. I could have kicked myself for being so self-absorbed, so unobservant, so naïve, so gullible. I had invited him up to my room. What was he to think?

Harry pulled out of the pocket of his coat a flattened oval tin of talcum powder. He smiled at me.

'Shall I powder you?'

'No, no, I think you'd better go.'

'Look,' he said, paying no attention to my protesting manner, and he unbuttoned and peeled back his shirt so it hung down behind him and bared his arms. He lifted his right hand to his head and flexed his right bicep. 'You can feel that. Hard as hell, man, go on.'

'I don't want to. I've got to work now. You'd better go. I don't want to do any of this,' I blurted.

'Of course you do. Like two peas in a pod we shall be – you can powder me now if you like.'

'No, no, please, not now,' I said realizing too late that it could mean I'd do it later. 'Please go,' I repeated, trying to get some insistence into my voice.

'I could stay the night. It's only my mum. Don't you go worrying about her. She won't mind, I often come to Cambridge and stay the night.' He gave a little laugh. 'She doesn't have a clue what we get up to.' He grinned, revealing the gap in his front teeth.

'No, look, I am not allowed to even call you in for coffee. The landlord, he'll call the police.'

Harry's face fell. It became long and drooping and lost its colour, becoming grey. He put his shirt back on. I had affronted his dignity. I didn't know how. Perhaps it was the mention of the police. He stood up and got his coat. He wasn't as tall as I had thought he was. In fact he was the same height as I was. Why did I think he was a giant of a man? How could I have seen him as such? He pulled a brush out of his coat pocket and brushed his hair. He put the sad talcum box away.

'You would call the police on me? After I fed your meter, you little puppy!'

He sat down and my relief at his signs of leaving turned back to panic. He started to take his coat off again and grinned.

'You were just testing, I know,' he said. 'You little tease!'

'No, please go now,' I said. 'I have to go somewhere, visit some people, they are expecting me,' I muttered and opened the door to my room and made as if to step out. 'Come on, please.'

I got to the landing, urging him to follow.

He came, sure enough, but now he was pleading.

'Tell them your friend's here. I'll pay for the phone. I'll walk you to the phone,' he said.

I heard the footsteps on the stairs. It wasn't the slow pace of my landlady. It was someone taking the stairs two at a time.

'Oi, didn't Mum say no guests?' It was the landlady's son, a man in his thirties with a bright shining round face. He looked up from the second floor landing and saw us.

'Oh, so that's the game, is it?' he said. 'A bit of bummery chummery for Christmas, eh? In my mum's house, eh? I'll give you a boot where you want tickling.' He was coming up the stairs when Harry, in complete panic, threw himself down the stairs in an attempt to run down past him. I stood paralysed on the landing. Harry got past the landlord's son with something of a scuffle, but the man got hold of the back of his coat and then kicked him in the pants pushing him head first down the stairs.

'I'm going, I'm going. It's only me, not him,' Harry shouted, struggling to get to his feet, panicked, breathless and, I hoped, with no broken ribs.

'I'll get you going,' the landlady's son shouted and took the stairs three at a time and got hold of Harry's coat from the back.

I ran down to where they were scuffling.

'We... he didn't do anything,' I shouted.

Harry got loose and ran out of the front door without shutting it behind him.

'Right, you are out,' the landlady's son said, out of breath now and turning to me.

'I don't know him. I didn't know what he ... he followed me from church,' I said.

'Church? You homos go to church?'

'Don't use that kind of language on me and I can't remember your mother saying I couldn't have anyone over for coffee.'

The landlady had come up to the hallway.

'He's right, Davey,' she said. 'I said no staying over and no women. He can stay the rest of the week what he's paid till.'

Davey gave me a dirty look and the two of them retreated to the basement.

'Let him be merry, Davey,' she said. 'It's Christmas and your pudding's on the boil.'

I was undecided as to what to do. I went up and got my coat and keys and walked out. The street was empty. I didn't tell myself why I was going, but I knew where. Outside the front door, my feet crunched the snow. The only sound.

I had never been propositioned by a man before, though in Poona, throughout my schooldays, I and the rest of the boys were aware that one or two of our teachers were inclined to sexual activity with boys whom they would seduce. I was a day scholar but at least half the school were boarders who lived in dormitories, some of them within the school grounds, one a converted army barracks a few hundred yards outside the grounds and another a converted bungalow donated by a philanthropic Parsi family. There would be stories of young boys returning long after hours at night to the dormitories from one of the masters' suite of rooms with slices of bread and jam as their reward.

In town there was also the spectral reputation or presence of a Pathan bakery owner called Ali Makroum who, it was said, roamed the streets on his bicycle wearing khaki shorts with a bag of cakes with which he tempted boys into his lair. I never came across Mr Makroum and didn't know anyone who had, but the myth and threat of being seduced by Ali was part of the lore of the town in that time. There was a jokey terror attached to the possibility of an encounter with him.

Then there were stories of boys in school who had been caught in bed together and punished by their housemasters with a public flogging which, far from meaning exposure and disgrace, became a badge of courage. Boys who entertained each other in sexual ways weren't thought of as unnatural in any way. Boys will be boys, until they moved on and were allowed access to girls. The homosexual teachers were different. They were recognized and characterized as dedicated 'homos'.

One of them was a maths teacher called Mr Wright, who wore three heavy rings on the fingers of his right hand. I thought of him as brilliantly and uniquely logical as he would demonstrate the solution of algebraic equations and geometric theorems on the blackboard in a way which to me illustrated the miracle of the obvious. He was very impatient with those in the class who were too lazy, inattentive, distracted or stupid to apply the demonstrated logic to solving the 'riders' or problems he would then set.

The school knew that there was no dodging the homework he would set after each class. The orange-covered maths exercise books had to be submitted the next school morning and piled on the master's desk. Mr Wright would ask one member of the class to bring the pile down to his rooms and wait with him while he corrected the books instead of filing off with the rest of the class to the daily morning assembly and prayers. In our class he would, because of my proficiency at his subject, pick me to deliver the books to his rooms, though I would find myself desperately hoping that he'd pick someone else.

'You have the questions, I want the answers,' he'd say to the class and add, 'tomorrow! Dhondy, fetch them to me in my rooms before the register is taken.'

I would of course say 'Yes sir' prompting the class to erupt each time in a murmur of 'Whey whey, whey!' What they were implying was that I was being summoned, recruited so he could fuck me.

The class would line up and troop off to assembly while I took the pile of books to his rooms at the end of one of the dormitories. I would find Wright sitting on an easy chair just within the doorway of his quarters drinking coffee and eating toast from a tray placed across the arms of the easy chair. I would wait with the pile of books for him to finish.

He had a pet parrot in a cage which hung from the ceiling above the easy chair and while Wright ate his breakfast the parrot would squawk and shout obscenities in Hindi and English. Wright would shout back in the raucous voice he reserved for Mitthu the parrot.

'Be quiet!' he would shout and then softly add, 'While I'm eating my toast!'

The ritual over, he would take the pile of books from me and correct them at an incredible speed. He'd glance at the pages in each notebook, seeming to take in the writing photographically. He would scribble ticks and crosses and throwing the book down, would move to the next one. It was my job to take the pile back and distribute the books and face some jibes from the more persistent of my classmates:

'Did he use Vaseline? Did you suck him off?' The jibes were best ignored.

Wright would turn up to teach and had, again incredibly, memorized how many sums, problems or riders each boy in the class had got wrong and one by one he'd call them up and slap them on the cheek with his thick rings – one slap for each wrong sum. His theory was that the pain would lead to a better effort next time.

What it did lead to was a demand for the exercise books of those, like myself, who got the right solutions each morning so they could be circulated and copied and then handed in. I and a few others were required, on pain of physical chastisement, to come to school early and pass our books around to be copied.

In all my time as Wright's favourite, he gave not the slightest indication of any sexual or physical inclination. I even began to doubt the rumour about him which said that he had turned homosexual after being jilted at the altar by a girl he loved.

I thought of Mr Wright and his hair parted in the centre like Harry's was. I got to the railway station through the deserted streets. Harry was sitting on a bench, the only person on the platform. I went up to him.

He stared at me for a few seconds and then turned away.

'If there's a pub open, we can go and have a drink,' I said. 'Before you catch your train, I mean.'

He shook his head. His cheek was bruised and was now apple red where the landlady's son had punched him.

'I am sorry about what happened,' I said.

'It wasn't your fault. I was looking for action and I got it. And I told you a lie. The train is not hours away. It'll come any minute.'

It did, and he left without another word.

I wrote a long letter to Mala that night. The snow, the church, anticipating Christmas Day, and Harry. I wrote of it as a bohemian encounter, refusing to commit to paper its triviality or my loneliness. I wanted to let her know that I was having the sort of time which helps a writer prepare.

At the end of the next term, when social life had become hectic with a crammed schedule, I returned to my room at the top of V staircase one day and was greeted on the landing by Berry Summers.

'There's a bloke says he's a friend of yours. Oldish geezer with parted hair. I said he could wait in my room.'

Berry was always restlessly pacing about and throwing balls to walls and catching them or punching the banisters just to harden his knuckles. Staying still wasn't something that would occur to him. He was curious and as we went up the stairs, I satisfied his curiosity. I told him about meeting Harry in the church and how he'd followed me home. I told him about the talcum powder and the home with his mother in King's Lynn. By the time we got to the top of the stairs, I knew I shouldn't have.

'I'll give him a cup of tea and get rid of him,' I said.

'No, you won't, he's not going into your room, bloody poofter,' Berry said. 'Fucking bum bandit, picking on you. I'll see him off. Unless you like him.'

A terror gripped my guts. I should have known that Berry would be as hostile as the wretched landlady's son. What was I to say to his question? Did I like him? I knew that any expression of sympathy would be an admission of affection. I hadn't even told him that I followed Harry to the railway station out of pity or sympathy or guilt for leading him on, however unintentionally and reluctantly. The cowardly male ego came to the fore. 'Of course I don't like him, the bastard!' And again, I knew I'd said the wrong thing.

Berry looked at me and nodded. He had from the first assumed a protective role towards me. Somewhere among his suppressed petty fantasies, I was the Indian in Billy Bunter's public school gang and as such had to be preserved from native predators.

'I'll give him a cup of coffee,' I said and walked into Berry's room.

Harry stood up with an uncertain smile.

'I found you. I remembered your first name and looked through all the college registers,' he said.

'This is my friend Berry,' I said, 'I am sorry I've forgotten your name.'

'Harry,' he said, stretching his hand out. Berry didn't take it.

'So you didn't give him the name of our college?' he asked me.

'Or my second name,' I said.

'Right, I can take care of your disgusting little friendship,' Berry said.

I wanted to intervene but immediately saw that Harry understood what was being said. He must have encountered a hundred such. He looked hunted. He made straight for the door without a word and Berry let him pass and then following him, landed a massive kick on his back, pushing him down the stairs. By the time Berry's kick connected Harry knew what was in store and he stumbled, but the foot connected to the small of his back and the impact of Berry's rugger-playing leg kicked him down one flight.

'No, let him go,' I shouted.

But Berry had tasted blood. Harry picked himself up, his

forehead bruised and with a possible bone or two broken, and scrambled for the next landing. Berry got there just behind him and kicked him again.

'Hold on, he's just come to say hello,' I said.

'Yeah hello and can I put my prick up your Indian bum. I know the sort. He's tried it out with the wrong person. Stay in King's Lynn, you fucking homo,' he shouted after Harry who reached the door to the quad and then stumbled and fell, holding his stomach.

I ran down the stairs past Berry now. I grabbed Harry by the elbow to help him up and he raised his other arm to ward off the blow he imagined I was about to land on his face.

'My God, why did you come here?' I asked. What else was I to say?

When he turned his face to me, his mouth was distorted and he was crying.

'Are you all right?' I asked.

Of course he wasn't all right. He pulled himself to his feet and, once again, to his seemingly diminished height. He pulled out a huge hanky and put it to his bruised forehead.

'Ah, innocent sheep to slaughter,' he said. 'Sheep to slaughter.'

Without a further word he dried his eyes and went. Shame was all I felt.

Berry wasn't in the least ashamed of what he had done. He boasted to the others in Hall how he'd seen off a queer who had come after me.

LAPIS LAZULI

AT EASTER, ENID said she was going to London to her parents and asked what I was doing. I said I suppose I'd pass the holidays in Cambridge as I had nowhere to go and I didn't have any money to do anything else. I might get to London and stay on my poet friend Adil Jussawalla's bedsit floor, but I couldn't impose on him for long. I'd call her when I got there.

'Do you fancy going to the Scilly Isles?' she asked.

'Where the hell are they and even if I did, how would I get there and what would I do?'

'They are off the tip of the west of Cornwall. You hitch rides from here, I'll hitch from London and I'll meet you at Penzance railway station at noon on the fourth. It'll take you maybe two days, but leave three and carry enough money to get to a bed-and-breakfast or a youth hostel in a town or village or in Penzance if you get there a day early. I'll pay for the rest. We'll loaf about Cornwall and get back in eight or ten days.'

She went off to London and I calculated backwards and set off one morning with my entire savings and that week's spending allowance. Enid had left me a map of England and indicated the route I could try and take. I walked to the west of Cambridge and stuck my thumb out at passing cars. A truck stopped and gave me a lift to Oxford.

I got several short lifts, some for only ten or twelve miles but I landed in Cirencester by the early evening. I thought I'd take Enid's advice and find a bed-and-breakfast for the night. I looked at the boards and found two addresses. I phoned them and was given directions from the town centre booth from which I'd phoned.

The bed-and-breakfast was in a modest terraced house with a green door. A sign in the window said 'B&B' and a sign below it said 'VACANCIES'. I rang the bell and a short, stocky, bald man in a vest answered the door.

'Phoned earlier. I ... er found the place quite easily using your directions.'

'Umm, there's no vacancy here. Full up, sorry.'

I pointed to the sign in the window.

'You heard me,' he said and slammed the door.

I stood in the street for a few moments and drew my breath. For the first time that day I felt isolated and even lost. And I was thinking, what if Enid thinks better of it, or finds other things to do and even if I get to Penzance, what if she doesn't turn up? I had her parents' phone number in London. Should I ring her?

I walked back to the town centre and looked for the roads leading to the west. I passed a sign saying 'Hotel'. Under it there was a board specifying the delights of the service and the tariff which was £3 a night for a single room. I walked on and having found a road that would eventually get me west and to Cornwall, put my rucksack down and stuck my thumb out.

Eventually a beige-coloured two-door MG stopped several yards in front of where I stood as though the driver had only decided to pick me up seconds after he passed me. I ran up to him and he opened the door leaning over the passenger seat with a grin.

'Get in lad. Where to?' he asked

'I'm trying to get to Penzance,' I said.

'Not going all that way but can take you beyond Exeter and get you well on the way.'

I thanked him and shut the door and he took off at speed.

He was in his forties perhaps. He wore a tweed jacket and had dark hair greased and neatly parted to the left.

'She's pretty nifty,' he said and then, grinning while anticipating his own joke, he added, 'I mean the car, not my wife.'

'Ah yes,' I said pretending to find it funny.

'So why Penzance? You don't look like a pirate. Aaarrrrhh!' He grinned again and turned his head.

'I've got a skull in my head and I've crossed my thigh bones,' I said, thinking it was the sort of banter he might appreciate.

'Very good, very good, a regular wag, eh? But seriously, what do you do?'

I told him.

'Ah, really? Indian? Wait, wait, wait, I've got something to show you.'

I didn't know what he meant. Was he going to point out some bit of landscape?

He was driving at a frightening speed now.

'India, hanh? Cambridge? Far away from home. You're going to appreciate this.'

'Good, I look forward to it,' I said.

'In this forest there's a parking space next to a picnic spot. See the flask in the back? Ovaltine! And some cheese crackers which the little lady has packed for me and thee!'

He drove on. It was still dusk and as the road passed through the forest there was very little light.

We came to the parking place and he stopped. He turned to me with a gleam in his eyes and his eyebrows went up and down. I felt a bit uneasy. He had talked about 'the wife' and the 'little lady' so I presumed he wasn't trying anything sexual.

'Now open that glove compartment, young Cambridge sahib, and what do you see?'

'The car manual, a ball point pen...'

'Put your hand in and pull it out.'

I did as he asked and pulled out a felt-covered jewellery box from the back of the glove compartment.

'Go on, open it,' he said.

I did. There was a blue stone in the shape of a twisted leaf. He turned the internal light on.

'Pick it up, have a good look,' he said, grinning proudly.

I examined the stone. It had faint white markings like the veins of a real leaf.

'Some precious or at least semi-precious stone. I am not very good on jewellery. Is it topaz or lapis lazuli?' I had to show interest.

'Maybe, but where is it from? Guess.'

'I haven't the faintest. A family heirloom?'

'You should know!'

'From the Lost City of Atlantis,' I said.

He took the stone from me.

'This,' he said, 'you won't believe, is a genuine piece of the Taj Mahal.'

I looked into his eyes to see if this was another feeble stab at humour.

'I was in India during the war and I pulled that out of the wall of the Taj Mahal with my penknife.'

'You actually stole that from the Taj Mahal?'

'Hey, steady on, Cambridge. What word did you use?'

'That is the most extreme act of vandalism I've ever heard of!' I said. I couldn't stop myself.

'Get the fuck out of my car,' he said.

I had already pressed the door handle and he began to push me out. If I hadn't fallen out, he would, I was convinced, have punched me in the face. He slammed the door, started the car and zoomed out on to the road.

The red back lights of the MG receded into the distance. I picked myself up. There was no traffic on the road and it was getting dark very fast. I started walking and then running down the road. If I could get beyond the forest I could at least see my way by moonlight. I was afraid. I didn't know of what but the episode had battered any courage I had. I ran, and walked when I couldn't run any more.

After what seemed hours, but was probably only minutes, the lights of a vehicle lit up the road. For a fleeting moment I thought I should stand in the middle of the road in his headlight and wave both hands in distress, but I didn't. Some sense of decorum or the fear that if the driver didn't want to stop he might run me over on this lonely spot stopped me. It had even occurred to me that in that seclusion, someone stopping a car in that manner might be up to no good or that the driver might, reciprocally, be wary of anyone hitching a ride in that lonely place. All that now flashed through my mind in an instant and I stood to the side and stuck out a polite begging thumb.

The van spotted me and stopped. I got in.

'How the hell did you get here?' The big gruff delivery driver in blue overalls asked me.

I told him the truth.

'Son of a jam tin,' he said.

He said he'd take me all the way to Penzance and I could sleep on a mattress he had in the back of the van if I was tired after all that.

He dropped me in the town. I was a day early. I found a B&B whose proprietor, a kindly white-haired widow, took me in for a charge of a few shillings. She was eager to tell me what I should see in Penzance and after wandering around all afternoon and evening I bought myself some fish and chips and returned to my billet. In the morning, I was given a huge breakfast and sure enough, there was Enid outside the ticket office at the stroke of noon. She gave me a long and intense kiss.

'More Lawrentian power struggles?'

'No,' she said. 'True love, of sorts.'

We bought tickets for the ferry which took us from Penzance to the Scilly Isles. We had no idea why we were there, except to be together.

We landed on St Mary's, the main island of the Scillies and walked around aimlessly till the evening.

Away from the jetty where the ferry brought us, the island seemed uninhabited. We had heard that Prime Minister Harold Wilson spent his holidays there and had a cottage somewhere on the island. Maybe we'd come across it.

We didn't. We wandered on to a farm as evening approached. We'd seen several haystacks in our wanderings and thought we'd spend the night on one of them under the stars.

We didn't have to. The woman who owned this particular farm spotted us while feeding her chickens and approached us. Was she going to tell us to get off her land?

She asked us what we were doing and when we told her, she invited us into her kitchen for a cup of tea and asked us where we planned to spend the night. We said we'd brought sleeping bags and would spend the night in the open somewhere. 'No, no, no, I wouldn't let you do that. There are haystacks in the barn there and you can spend your nights there; there's a tap and an outdoor toilet,' she said, 'and of course come in for a cup of tea in the morning.'

'Thank you,' we both said.

'I tell you what,' she said, 'my farmhand has gone sick and I could do with a bit of help. You can have breakfast here if you'll wake up and fill the buckets for the animals.'

It was a deal.

We slept in the hay on top of our sleeping bags so we could cuddle up to each other. In the dark Enid stripped.

'Feeling shy?'

'Not at all,' I said and took my clothes off.

We made love in the haystack which proved a very shaky bed, collapsing under our weight with every turn. Besides, hay seems to stick to the skin and it took a brushing to get it off and stop itching.

'Can't remember if Mellors and Lady Chatterley had a tumble in the hay,' Enid said. 'Great, but not recommended.'

After four nights we made our way together back to London. I didn't see Enid for the rest of the holiday, though both of us were in London. She had determined, she later told me, to stay aloof.

ON CUMBALLA HILL

IT WAS SOME weeks into the term before my mind turned to Richard John Barter Snow. I had met him, or encountered him in passing, in Bombay, and we'd agreed to meet in Cambridge.

My sweetheart Mala had been shipped off to that great and bewildering city from the cloistered confines of the much smaller Poona where we had met and paired up. Her father was a lieutenant general in the army and besides being divorced and having the custody of two daughters, he had in those days a war to fight against China. He didn't have too much time to spare for his daughters and the inattention allowed our affair to flourish.

We both knew that if he wasn't flying off to Delhi for conferences with Nehru and the defence minister, he would be in Ladakh in charge of a front in the Sino-Indian war of 1962. If he was in Poona and if he had had the time to keep an eye on his daughter, or make an assessment of me, he would certainly have disapproved.

The next best thing, to keep her out of mischief, her father must have thought, was to send her to a residential 'ladies' college away from Poona. She was enrolled in the Sophia Convent atop a hill in South Bombay, a good choice because her divorced mother, who lived there with her new husband, could now take her in hand.

My mission became to get to Bombay, a hundred and twenty miles and four hours down the western hills of the Deccan plateau by train from our town. There was plenty to do in Bombay for me at that time. I had graduated from my Indian college in Poona and the letter offering me a place at Cambridge had arrived. All the scholarship interviews were held in Bombay and that's where tickets, passports, visas, bookings for the boarding houses of South Kensington and Earls Court were to be negotiated.

In Bombay, I'd sleep on the floor of my uncle's flat and visit Mala at her institution and she would escape the watchful eye of the nuns or get a legitimate 'exeat' and come out with me to neck in my uncle's rickety Fiat 1100 parked in some quiet corner by the Bombay seafront. Experienced friends told me that the best place to park and carry on was directly under a lamp post and not at the mid-point between lamp posts, because their light would render us visible to the prying eyes of perverts and blackmailing policemen bicycling by.

The University term in England opened in October and in the monsoon of June and July of 1964 I was making the last arrangements for departure. I had taken Mala out for lunch. She had to be back in college that afternoon as she was under strict surveillance having been caught AWOL the previous week. As I left her in the porch, it began to rain, the heavy monsoon downpour which comes down in sheets and very soon turns the narrow hill roads, winding between stone parapets, into rapid and slippery streams. A taxi emptied its cargo of nuns in the porch of the college and as it turned around to descend Cumballa Hill, I hailed it. I told the taxiwallah I was going to town.

We went cautiously down the hill. The rain was relentless. I hadn't seen anyone on the road, but the driver chatting in Bombay's crude Hindustani said, 'White son of a bitch. Bastards thought they owned the place; now look at him, like a drowned rat. He tried to book me on my way up, but you got there first. Let him soak.'

I saw him. A white man with his trousers futilely rolled up to his knees, the fast running water swirling round his ankles, with an umbrella that did very little to shelter him from the punishing rain.

'Go on, stop for him,' I said, seeing the man trying to wave the cab down.

'You pay, you say,' said the driver and stopped.

John Snow got in, furling his umbrella. His white shirt was transparent grey, soaked and sticking to his nipples.

'Where are you going?' It was an offer.

'Apollo Bunder,' he said. That was near the docks.

'I'm going that way, I'll drop you,' I said.

He was very quiet so I asked him if he was a sailor. He said he wasn't but didn't volunteer what he was. The journey would take longer than half an hour so I persisted. He was English, he had been teaching for a year in the hills in northern India, his aunt was one of the nuns at Sophia and he had been visiting her. Now he was off, back to England for his first term at University.

'Which one?'

'Cambridge,' he said.

'Something of a coincidence? I'm going there too,' I said.

It wasn't what he expected to hear, but he began to grin, a very stained-tooth yellow grin, reluctant and ironic.

'Which college?' he asked and I knew he was testing me out to see if I was telling the truth.

'Pembroke,' I said.

'Look me up at Queen's,' he said.

We exchanged names and said we'd meet, underplaying our surprise at the odds that had brought us together in a taxi in South Bombay, before he unfurled his umbrella and stepped into the filthy, flowing flood of the city's monsoon streets wading through the floating garbage and dead rats which now came to the surface.

I told Mala and my aunt and uncle about the strange encounter. I didn't need to write his name down. It was clear and memorable. But when I thought of John Snow on my first day at Cambridge, I couldn't remember which college he was at. The game of being casual had allowed it to slip from my mind. I was sure I'd find him, though. We were, after all, both reading Natural Sciences.

Looking down the names of colleges, I was sure he'd said Queen's and so I went in search of him. I found someone called R.J.B. Snow and deduced that the J must be the John. Indians hardly ever had three names and even if they did, they didn't use the second one. I found his rooms. He wasn't there the first few times I tried, but finally I found him. He opened the door to me and said, 'Bombay! What was your name again?'

He shared the rooms with Dave, a man who boasted, without provocation, that he wanted to be labour prime minister one day and had, from the first week, joined the University Labour Party and volunteered for activities in it. Dave came from a working-class family from a small industrial town in Yorkshire. His father was a miner and his grandfather had been one. Dave was the first of his family to have gone to a grammar school and by dint of his academic achievements he had won a scholarship to Cambridge.

This was the literary era of the 'kitchen sink' writers whose plays and novels were about the transition and tensions generated when boys and girls of the working class pushed themselves through getting into grammar school and gaining entrance to universities into the professions and into politics. The literature dramatized the conflicts of the new meritocracy.

Dave was almost a caricature of such a character. He was a lanky lad with curly ginger hair and thick spectacles which he constantly took off and cleaned with his handkerchief while he talked. It was his boast that both his grandfathers hadn't learnt to read.

In the coming weeks, as Johnny and I hung out together, Dave was full of the defeats they had inflicted on the 'bloody Tories' in the Cambridge Union (the University's debating society) votes and in other forums of which I had never heard. He talked endlessly of the alliances that had to be made with 'Trots, Communist Party members, anarcho-syndicalists, anarchists and even liberals'. The deals always seemed devious and he seemed proud to be privy to this big game in town, making alliances with one group one week and 'ditching' them when the opportunity arose. He carried this on with the assiduity with which the more sexually successful undergraduates acquired and abandoned girlfriends. He was determined to build up the momentum to go back north, from whence he came, after University and to climb the pole by standing as a town councillor in his small mill town and then offering himself as the locally born and bred candidate for election to Westminster and beyond.

Dave asked me about my political affiliations and I said I didn't quite have a label for them, but had been introduced to the works of Marx and Lenin. I said I was certainly anti-capitalist but didn't have any time for Stalin.

'Ah, don't be too hasty about Comrade Stalin,' he said. 'Cruel to a minority in the service of the majority.'

'Even his daughter didn't like him,' Johnny said, to which Dave just grinned vacantly as he wiped his specs.

John Snow and I met most days. He would borrow a Pembroke gown and eat in our hall, unnoticed by the serving staff as an intruder. We stayed up late very many nights, after the college gates had shut, listening to the records he'd bought and which everyone was listening to – the Beatles and the Stones. He bought everything Bob Dylan, Joan Baez and Pete Seeger had ever put out. Apart from that he had some obscure folk records, one of which, sung in a Scottish accent, went like:

If it wes'ne fer the weavers
Whet would we do?
We wouldna ha' cleeth, either oo woo

Everyone knew 'The times they are a changing' but only the two of us knew 'If it wes'ne fer the weavers'.

With the song of the weavers and the rest, we drove the future PM, who shared the study with John but had his own bedroom, quite mad. He wasn't used to comings and goings throughout the night, but now that he was paired in a room with a public school man with a weird Indian friend, he put it down to one side of Cambridge he had come there to learn.

It was the pressures of his ambitions rather than our petty harassment that drove Dave crazy. Literally. He began imagining things, hearing voices. At first he was counselled, then detained and certified. We cycled miles to the mental hospital to which he had been sent, sure that he would soon be out and resume his ambitious journey to 10 Downing Street. It was only when we saw him, his face puffed up and his eyes glazed, that we knew the game was up. He wouldn't come back, not to the University and not to the ambition and path he had chalked out for it. That path would take him, he used to say, through the Cambridge Labour Party into a northern constituency, into parliament and then, by the eighties, into 10 Downing Street. Who, apart from Dave, was thinking that far?

He was full of the rhetoric of the times. All my friends and acquaintances were against the American presence in Vietnam. Dave's rhetoric about this war concentrated on the Labour Party's attitude towards America. It wasn't even about Britain's foreign policy. He didn't follow the events of the war, the American invasion of neighbouring Laos and Cambodia, but very closely studied the ups and downs of the Labour Left's battle with the Labour Right.

His politics were about class. The rich must be dispossessed, the workers must control Britain. When he talked of the utopia the Labour Party would herald in when he became an MP and climbed the ladders of power, his eyes would glaze over. Dave's illness filled me with a new kind of fear. Here was a lad with a very clear idea of what he wanted his life to be. He seemed to have planned it year by year and he had this burning purpose to bring social justice to British society and to humble the rich and powerful by gaining power himself. All derailed now. Was it this obsessive ambition itself that had driven him to his breakdown?

It made me think that I had no parallel plan, no ambition apart from the vague idea that I wanted to be a writer of some sort. It seemed as remote an ambition as Dave's charted course to be the prime minister. And yet I had the feeling that I could perhaps get there. After all Dom Moraes had won an Oxford poetry prize a few years previously and someone called V.S. Naipaul was becoming famous and controversial through his fiction and factual books.

I hadn't confessed any such ambition to my family. My father, with his military bent of mind, would not have seen it as a sensible career path. Yet the ambition came to me when in Bombay, sitting in trams or in my room in my grand-uncle's flat, I read Lawrence Durrell's *Alexandria Quartet*. If he could construct a fabulous plot interwoven in four novels around the city of Alexandria, why couldn't I do the same for exotic Bombay?

But did I know enough about Bombay to dream up, or represent in plausible avatars, characters who would hold a reader's attention through a set of novels? I would have to return to India and immerse myself in its life as perhaps Durrell did in Alexandria or Albert Camus did in Algeria. But where would I live and how would I earn money to sustain a bohemian life?

THE LOCALE OF AMBITION

AT A SECOND-HAND bookstall in Cambridge Market I picked up a paperback entitled *Miguel Street* by V.S. Naipaul. I had read his essays in *Encounter in India* and his book of discovery in India but this was the first fiction of his I had come across. I read it avidly and then searched for other fictional writing by him in the library.

I realized as I read more of his work that he had turned his back on his native Trinidad. He lived in England and wrote his books of travel and discovery from his base here.

I had also read a book by Dom Moraes called *Gone Away* in which he seemed to say that he had left India and developed his talent as a poet and writer only as a consequence of doing so.

It was bewildering. Did one have to come away to write anything of value? On the one hand the immersion in the familiar seemed to have inspired Naipaul's books. They were surely about the people he knew or observed in Trinidad. His characters in his fiction were certainly based upon his family. So did one need the distance of time and space to turn experience and observation into fiction?

Would I too have to 'go away' to become a real writer? The question initiated bouts of nostalgia. Of course I would have to return to India, but that very thought inspired a certainty.

Walking alone along the water meadows of the Cam in the evenings brought it home in the form of a question.

Why did India close down for me? Why did I come away? Because India became oppressive and there were no roots to which to cling, no roots that clutched. There was no ancestral home. The house that my aunts lived in, where I was brought up, was a series of five rooms that followed one on the other, like railway compartments with through doors, rented from the neighbours who had an identical house, Siamese-twinned down the spine with ours. My 'room' in this house was the end portion of a side veranda, shut off from the rest of it by my book cupboard that served as a partition. The rest of the veranda was used to hang clothes to dry in the monsoons, and the far end of it had old trunks with musty and moth-eaten clothes and boots in them, stuff that had been discarded but never thrown away.

As children, my sister, cousins and I would pull out the old clothes and wear them for a dressing-up game – the khaki peaked caps with badges which my aunts wore in the Woman's Auxiliary Corps India (the WACI) during the Second World War, the discarded striped woollen trousers with braces that my grandfather wore when he was 'in service' as a clerical officer in the Land Records Office, old saris with burns and tears and moth-eaten holes in them. Their damp smell was tolerable when they were worn and partially aired; they made you sick when for a laugh the others thrust your face in the suitcase and held it down, letting you go if you coughed and were on the point of throwing up.

The houses that my parents lived in were rented to them by the army and every three or four years my father was transferred and my parents relocated to another town or army encampment in India. The nomadic existence may have been interesting for my parents at first, but as they grew older the adventure of moving all one's possessions, relocating, making new friends and acquiring new routines became a chore, the regrettable side of 'being army'.

It left me with no base and no direction to follow in, except the general idea that I would have to acquire, like everyone else in my family, a profession. No one in my family had ever been in business and there was an unspoken snobbery against buying and selling things at whatever level. Banias, the merchant Hindu castes, did that. Besides, business needed capital and I don't think anyone in my family had seen more than the amount it took to buy a second-hand car.

This lack of a home and direction didn't resolve itself into thoughts and words. It was unease, an absence. But there were frustrating presences. Growing up in India in those days meant growing up surrounded by poverty and irrational belief, however beautiful and traditional some of it was. As a child one doesn't shut one's eyes to poverty. I wanted to know why people we saw weren't eating, why they were thin, diseased, maimed, begging. I wanted to know where they went at night and what they did in the mornings. And from where they got their next meal and from whence they derived hope. There were no answers.

The dreadful dimension of poverty was the famine, flood, earthquake and drought that were constantly with us, killing and devastating the poor, leaving the rich untouched. God was doing that. God was the root of the irrational. Somehow this faith was inextricably tied up with the inequality, the poverty and the seeming indifference of the entire country to it.

I was taught the Zoroastrian prayers, rituals and doctrines at the age of six. It was a pious household in which prayers to Ahura Mazda were loudly declaimed and the servant went around twice a day with a burning censer of sandalwood, passing it through the rooms and offering it to each person in the household who would interrupt whatever they were doing for a second and join their hands in respect to the fire. Why respect fire? Because it was energy and the symbol of God.

By the time I was thirteen, I was ready to denounce religion and declare myself an atheist. By the time I was fourteen, I was, in spirit, a communist and used to keep company with one Aspy Khambatta, a young man, six or seven years older than myself, who lived in our neighbourhood and had set himself up as the intellectual scourge of hypocrisy and superstition. The Soviet Publishing House sold the works of Marx, Lenin and Stalin for the price of a cup of tea. Aspy bought them and read the most obscure chapters to me and my friends. It was a matter of pride to me that I knew what Lenin had said to the Second Conference of the United Soviets of Agricultural Workers and that the elders of my family didn't have a clue. They knew, however, that I had picked up the rhetoric from 'Lenin' as Aspy was called when he grew a little wispy beard.

Aspy was unusual. He lived with his stubbly, hunchbacked mother and his equally unattractive sister in two rooms in a house on the opposite side of the street from us. The house had been divided in three, Aspy's family to the left, my friend Dara Cama's family in the middle and a man who showed films to the armed forces with a portable projector and had a wife who was suspected of wantonness, in the third.

Aspy had blue eyes and blonde hair. His Parsi father had acrimoniously left his mother, causing a minor scandal in the town when Aspy was born. The couple used to run The English Bookshop on East Street in Poona Cantonment, the British Raj part of town. Aspy's mother would serve the soldiers who came to browse and she made friends with them, which set her a cut above the rest of the women in our neighbourhood. She spoke to Britishers; not real 'sahibs', just soldiers, my aunts said. She was a tradeswoman, they added a little snobbishly, and entertained these soldiers at her bookshop after hours, it was rumoured, on Sundays. She struck up a liaison with an English sergeant and her third child was born looking very white and, to his father, very suspect.

The father noisily quit the home and she brought the boy up on her own, finding it extremely difficult to make ends meet. She insisted that he was his father's child, and never retracted or confessed. She even got a pliant priest, when Aspy was six or seven, to try and initiate him into the Zoroastrian faith. When this initiation ceremony was in progress, his mother's husband, the cuckolded Parsi, turned up with a gang of bigots and picketed their home with black flags and slogans.

It was only in my teenage years that my aunt told me this secret of the neighbourhood. By this time I was well on the way to being a disciple and a communist and it strengthened my antagonism to religion and gave me a moral point to ponder – so what if Aspy was an English sergeant's son? Accidents of birth determined, or should determine, nothing.

His mother, a virtual outcast of the neighbourhood, referred to as *butki*, a word meaning 'shorty' but carrying with it the contempt reserved for those who are damned to smallness, would come and visit at our house just before dinner time. My aunts would feel obliged to ask her to eat with us. It became a routine and they resented it and complained out of earshot about it. Even we, the children of the house and our friends, very many of whom were her neighbours, became aware that dinner in our household would be delayed by minutes and finally by the hour in a waiting game to see if she would take the hint and go. It was an unspoken game of hunger and shame, with her sitting tight and making small talk and my aunts, resentful that they were being taken advantage of, not having the courage to blow the game and ask her to go and not to return at mealtimes.

I didn't want to be at the collective table for those dinners, though it was the custom of the house that we ate together, come what may. It made me lose my appetite. It made my heart shrink when once I saw her, just as my aunts went to wash their hands after the meal, thinking she was unobserved, putting bits of food she grabbed from the leftovers into her sari to take home to her son. Pride and the swallowing of it. I didn't want to know. I wanted to be where it didn't exist.

Aspy was academically smart and was put through college by his working sister and was going to sit for the Union Public Service Commission exams which recruited a very few boys and girls, after they had graduated from one of India's universities, to the elite Indian Administrative Service.

His mother couldn't afford the newspapers, which were delivered to our veranda each morning for my septuagenarian grandfather. It was his habit to finish with the papers and then pile them in a neat stack on top of his cupboard. It was his little hoard which he would sell to the waste-paper women who would come round with baskets, soliciting tin cans, empty bottles, paper and any other exhausted or disposable objects for which they would pay small sums of money.

Aspy lumbered up one day in his rubber slippers and asked my grandfather if he could, each afternoon, after my grandfather had finished with them, borrow the daily newspapers. Grandfather was sitting at his trestle table in the front veranda of our house, arranging his stamp collection in his albums. He readily agreed. Though determinedly indifferent to the disputes of the neighbourhood, he knew that Aspy and his mother had suffered at the hands of an unforgiving but hypocritical morality. He was on Aspy's side.

Aspy would make two trips each day to borrow the papers and then to return them. We all knew that Aspy resented bowing and scraping and saying thank you each day he had to borrow the papers.

He was quite eccentric. For example, he would, in no particular context, confront the strangers who passed him on the pavement where he strode past, with a cry of 'Crises, crises, look at the closing prices!'

He had religious uncertainties, crises of a faith he didn't even acknowledge he possessed. He would confess to 'moments of doubt' which would make me feel that he was suffering the agony of Christ in the wilderness. He confessed to us that he masturbated several times a day and the main temptation, the distraction that lured him to this wasteful and exhausting evil, was the young maidservant who came to clean and wash for his neighbours. She was, he said, quite unjustly, a slut and a whore; he knew by the way she looked at him that she knew he was wasting his seed on the wind with the image of her before him. He said she was a temptress and aware of her power but she didn't strike me or my friends as a Salome. It wasn't to Lenin but to Jesus Christ that Aspy prayed for deliverance from this debilitating obsession. He told us he had other sex objects in mind and they were the old and young women of the neighbourhood, but we enquired no further lest they turned out to be our aunts, sisters or mothers, whose honour we would then be called on to defend, even against the masturbatory fantasies of the religious revolutionary.

Aspy was full of stories of Rasputin and his hold over the corrupt Romanov Tsarina. When he told them, you could see the envy in his eyes. He would have loved to be able to cultivate such hypnotic power and use it on a rich woman. He was torn between the mania for religion and the redeeming fires of communist revolution which would wipe out morality and hypocrisy and suffering from India. He couldn't resolve the dilemma, this conflict between the great myths that dominated his contrary way of apprehending the world. It was my first encounter with a person struggling with contradictory passions of such strength – abstract passions at that – with their roots in his poverty and needless shame.

One day, as I passed him on my way back from school, standing at his usual vantage point, watching the neighbourhood from behind the waist-high white parapet of his tiny front yard, he motioned to me.

'Stalin is dead,' he said.

I was unmoved by the news but tried to compose a face of condolence. He had obviously been affected by the news.

'In 1917 Stalin said, "There is no God". In 1953, God said, "There shall be no more Stalin".'

One night at dinner, with my grandfather, two aunts, my sister and me at table, my older aunt declared that we should eat but that she was fasting that day. I asked why, and she gave me a reason. It was a particular tribute to the Zoroastrian dead.

'Your fasting won't bring them to life,' I said.

The adults let the comment pass and asked me to finish my spinach.

'I hate it. Maybe I'll go on the fast myself. Help the dead along a bit.'

My grandfather looked up.

'Get on with your food. And be respectful. This is our religion you're mocking.'

'Religion is the opiate of the masses,' I said, quoting the phrase in English.

'What was that?'

I repeated it.

'I know who's been teaching you all this and even that is wrong. What you mean is "opium", there's no such word as "opiate".' My grandfather was emphatic. He tried out the phrase himself: "Religion is the opium of the masses."'

'It's Karl Marx.'

'It's ignorant rubbish. There is no such word. That Lenin of yours should learn to speak English before he goes around perverting little boys. And when you see him tell him he hasn't brought yesterday's papers back. Opiate. Bloody fool.'

The next morning when I reported my act of defiance, Aspy asked to borrow my grandfather's dictionary. I was to smuggle it out as best I could. I did, and there the word was – 'opiate'. Aspy said my grandfather was an arrogant fool and when the revolution came would have to be eliminated for the citizen's crime of being uncomradely in his criticisms. I didn't like that. I planned to be in that vanguard of the revolution, but not in order to eliminate my grandfather. Fair enough, he had made a mistake over a word which sounded obscure enough, but then he was kind enough to lend his newspapers when he'd finished with them. I didn't tell Aspy that. He wouldn't have taken kindly to it.

But he was intent on rubbing my grandfather's nose in the limitations of his English vocabulary. The next day when he came to pick up his newspapers, I was on the veranda reading comics. He looked at the headlines.

'The Pope is visiting India and these fools, even if they are not Christians, will flock to touch the hem of his garment. Religion is the opiate of the masses. It's in the dictionary.'

My grandfather knew that the admonishment was meant for him. The next day he took the newspapers indoors when he'd finished reading them and retired early for his afternoon nap so that when Aspy came to collect them, the veranda was deserted, the table folded up, the chairs put away, and the door to the front room padlocked.

My grandfather must have relented after a few hours because he called me to his bed.

'I brought these in by mistake today. I am getting absent-minded,' he said, his thin ankles and shins showing through his white pyjamas. 'Take these papers to your friend Jesus Christ or Lenin or whatever he is today.'

I took the papers over.

'The bourgeoisie will stew in their own guilt,' Aspy said.

Aspy passed the Public Service Entrance exams with flying colours. The access to newspapers had been invaluable, he said; his mother sent a tray of sweets she had made with a thank you note on the day his results were announced. He went to train as an Indian administrator, was given his first wage and came back on holiday wearing well-tailored shirts and suits. He had turned nationalist during his year or so away and he now sought out the café company of older and employed people, avoiding his erstwhile disciples.

When we finally got him to ourselves, he made it clear that communism could only exist in the most advanced capitalist countries and that India must now make do with socialism. He implied that he was critical of Nehru and the Indian government but was not now at liberty to say in which particular he disagreed with them. He was a civil servant and would soon hold the position of a Deputy Collector, the sole power running a district for the government. He'd changed. He had money in his pocket.

Six months later, having assumed a post as Assistant Collector of some remote district, he returned to Poona and to his mother's little flat. He went to Dorabjee's, our town's most renowned departmental store, and looked in the display cases of the food section and the gifts counter and the electronics department. A year before that and more he wouldn't have ventured into Dorabjee's. It was not the sort of shop that his mother could afford. The proprietors, a well-known Parsi society family in our town, greeted him respectfully and he smiled and sneered back. Now the dogs would deign to recognize him, would they? Half an hour later he invited me and another friend to come with him. He called on the local Superintendent of Police. He was using his new authority to order the police to raid Dorabjee's and arrest them for contravening import regulations and keeping smuggled cheese, tobaccos, electronics, perfumes and the rest.

The police raided Dorabjee's that evening. It caused a stir in the town. There had never been such an incident or such an order from someone who, as a civil magistrate, had the power to instruct the police. They found no smuggled goods. The stuff Aspy had seen earlier had vanished from the shelves and the display cases. The police, who knew which side their bread was buttered, had tipped them off.

Aspy had been naïve. His newfound position and power went to his head. He wanted revenge on the rich of the town who had ostracized his mother. It struck me that he may even have wanted revenge on our unoffending family, because his mother, no longer in need of free dinners, came round one day in a new sari and asked for my nineteen-year-old sister's hand for her son who was now settled in a good job. My sister couldn't believe that it was not a joke. The thought of marrying 'Lenin' unsettled her and she cried and vomited in the basin on the back veranda. My aunts reassured her. They had only said they would put the proposal to our parents out of politeness. They would have to mention it to Mum and Dad but they would certainly add that it was a ridiculous idea. They genuinely thought it was an absurd proposition and attributed it to Aspy trying to win the most-sought-after status symbol in the neighbourhood and in half of Poona. My sister didn't need the flattery. She knew she was.

Aspy didn't marry anyone in India. We heard he'd gone to Delhi as an officer in the central civil service's Labour Bureau. As their most able man, they sent him to a university in America to pick up a qualification in labour relations.

We, his erstwhile disciples, discussed his progress and his transformation from the bitter misfit to the bright young man of the Indian Administrative Service. The night before he left, I was returning from my evening ramble on my bicycle and he shouted out to me from where he was leaning on the whitewashed curved-top shallow wall that separated his house from the gutter that ran past it along the street.

'So the USA, then?' I asked.

'Listen, you! We all know you think you're damned smart and this world is too small for you. It was too small for me and I've got out. Maybe you are right; take my advice and get out too.'

'I'll think about it,' I said. He pointed a finger to the sky in a token I didn't understand and turned and went into his house.

He never came back from the USA. He defected and married, it was said in our neighbourhood, an American lady dentist. He quit the Indian Administrative Service, became an American citizen, sent for his mother and sister, settled in provincial America, changed his name and became a born-again Christian.

Years later, his mother sent my aunts, who had been kind to her, a letter, which they were proud to receive with its United States postage stamps on the envelopes. She had signed the letter with 'May the blessings and mercy of the Lord Jesus Christ grace your lives and household.'

GENTLEMEN DON'T WEAR BROWN SUITS

IT WAS WHEN I realized, in my last year of college in Poona, that all my friends seemed to be planning to settle into professions or join their fathers' businesses that I began thinking of what I would do with my life. My father would have wanted me to join the army or navy. The fact that I was short-sighted would mercifully rule that out. I wasn't, as my first cousins were, the tough athletic sort.

Poona was still a small town with more colleges than manufacturing enterprises. I couldn't think of a career in either. The town would stifle me, I arrogantly thought. Distancing myself from India, from the social circles I knew, from the disgust at the poverty, muddle and superstition that was all around, became a slow, nagging obsession. There was no way of getting away except to get a scholarship to study and admission to a university abroad.

I considered going to Russia and spoke to a girl who had qualified as a doctor there. She said that the studies were good, but the people were bad. She also said I'd have to learn Russian for two years before I could even think of studying anything else, that no one in the Soviet Union believed in communism and that almost everyone she'd met wanted to go and live in America, to own jeans and washing machines and have TV with Mickey Mouse on it. When I told her why I wanted to go abroad, she said she understood but that I shouldn't exchange one form of confinement for another. I wrote to a couple of American universities but couldn't make sense of the courses they offered.

My one act of dereliction was, two years before graduating from university in Poona, at the age of sixteen, to have run away from a college of chemical engineering which I attended for all of one term and hated and truanted from. The college was in Bombay, my army parents were in Delhi and I left Poona to take up a much-coveted place in this college. I was lodged with a grand-uncle, my grandfather's brother who was a widower and kept a musty flat in central Bombay.

He was called Rustom, known in the family as Russi Kaka. He had dedicated his life to Gandhian principles, wearing only handspun cotton, eating only vegetarian food and distributing a few hundred umbrellas in the slums as an act of annual charity.

He would venture forth in one of the vans of the soap factory he owned, supported by a couple of servants who carried the umbrellas and walked behind him through the mud and mire of the monsoon shanties, distributing them to the occupants of the hovels. His daughter, who visited, fought with him. It was misplaced charity. She knew for a fact that the wretches to whom he gave them sold them to a trader, who followed this comic entourage, buying the umbrellas up for a song.

'At least they got a song,' Russi Kaka would reply.

He would tell me stories of running an amateur ambulance during the freedom struggle in which the non-violent followers of Gandhi occupied the streets by squatting in them and were removed by baton-wielding police who'd smash their heads, beat and arrest them. He and his crew would take the casualties with smashed heads, broken shins and bruised faces and bodies to the makeshift infirmaries, driving their private cars draped with bed-sheets on which they painted red crosses.

He was proud of his yoga and of the very thin master who came to practise it with him. He would swallow a three-foot taper and pull it out again, soiled with bile and vomit, 'in order to clean the food passage to the stomach'. The *piece de resistance*, which I did not witness, but of which he boasted, was ingesting fluids up his penis, starting with oils and graduating through curds to mercury. Russi Kaka said he hadn't reached the ultimate stage, but his master was the world expert at this particular skill.

I stopped attending the lectures and spent my time in Bombay reading paperbacks I could buy or borrow. Anything and everything, from cheap Westerns by Max Brand and Zane Grey, through Lawrence Durrell's fascinating, irreverent *Alexandria Quartet* and travel books, to Waugh, Dostoevsky, Camus, and then Marx and the tracts and lectures of Lenin.

Apart from the romance of *Brideshead* which introduced me to a wistful Oxford, I read Forster's *Longest Journey*, partly set in Cambridge, and then a slim Penguin by Anthony Sinclair about contemporary Cambridge in which women were referred to as 'totties', which conveyed the idea of boundless freedom.

My reading took me into worlds and modes of thought which I knew none of my friends or family were acquainted with or, I thought, would appreciate. What I took away from books such as Camus' *The Outsider* or *The Fall* was that my rejection of religions and my evaluation of social injustice made me something of an 'existentialist'. I struggled to get a clear definition of the word and fuelled by adolescent conceit thought I was edging towards the 'amorality' of Camus' characters. There were a couple of friends with whom I could discuss these conceits but the reaction of the others would have been a complete blank.

When I left Chemical Engineering College in Bombay and landed in Delhi, my parents were not pleased. I had proved myself ungrateful for all the privileges I had been afforded. Over the days I made a deal with Mum and Dad. I would return to Poona and lodge at my aunts' again and resume the Bachelor of Science course, specializing in Physics in which I was interested. Then we'd talk about a career.

I spent a few months in Delhi reading everything I could lay my hands on and then rejoined college in Poona. By this time the idea of a British university – and I knew only of Oxford and Cambridge – was firmly in my mind.

I worked hard, studying through the night and sleeping for four or five hours in the early morning before solving more maths, physics and chemistry past-exam papers. I sat for the exams, waited a few months for the results, did well and wrote for admission to several universities abroad. One seemingly miraculous day I received a letter from Pembroke College saying they would accept me. I had, of course, to find a means of paying for my three years at Cambridge, something my father couldn't begin to afford and so I applied to the Tata Endowment for the Higher Education of Indians. I got a letter in due course inviting me for an interview.

There was only one interviewer. She was the director of the Tata Endoment and seemed to be the sole determinant of my future. She was in charge of handing out and administering the funds for boys and girls who wanted to study abroad. The scholarship paid one's fees and a very meagre sum in expenses and pocket money besides. A part of the sum allocated to each scholar was regarded as a loan and had to be returned to the Foundation when one had completed one's studies and had gained employment. This was a material and spiritual requirement. The Foundation wanted its scholars to feel that one generation was assisting the next.

The director's name was Mrs Vesugarh. She was an old wrinkled Parsi lady with the slightly hooked nose of our race and a shock of white hair. My first sight of her startled me because I mentally remarked her resemblance to the portrait of Bertrand Russell on the dust jacket of his *History of Western Philosophy* which I happened to be reading and was carrying with me to assist with what I thought was my intellectual pose.

Once I had caught a glimpse of her, I thought she might make the comparison herself if she saw the photograph and that might blow the whole interview off course, so I kept the book on my lap. After shaking her hand, I sat opposite her across a huge mahogany desk.

'What's that book you're carrying around?' I showed it to her.

'He is not good on Hegel,' she said and handed the book back. The photograph of Russell passed her by. If it hadn't, she could have been looking at a slightly distorting mirror but she wouldn't, of course, have noticed the resemblance. I said I hadn't got to Hegel yet, but she was intent on telling me how she had once met Russell and had tea with him.

She finished the anecdote and abruptly asked me, 'Why Cambridge?' She was looking at the forms I had filled in and the two pages of autobiography I had had to write.

'I suppose one would meet with the best minds in the world in the field of natural science.'

'Nonsense,' she said emphatically. 'There are good brains everywhere. The reason you go to Oxford or Cambridge is to make the contacts that will serve you for the rest of your life.'

I could only agree that this would be a good reason to go but she wasn't interested in my response.

'You see that door there, that's the lavatory. Go and use it.' Her tone had compelling authority and she was going to sign my scholarship. I went. I told myself it was like the doctor asking you to produce a sample.

When I emerged, she sat me down again and began chatting.

'We are going to equip you with some clothes tomorrow. The tailor will be here and you'd better be here to get measured at ten o'clock.'

So she was virtually telling me that they were going to clothe me and send me off, which surely meant I had passed whatever test she intended. 'You are wondering what all that was about?'

'Yes ma'am, I was.'

'I wanted to see if you pulled the flush. You passed.' She smiled for the first time. 'And Mr Dhondy, you do eat with a knife and fork and use a side plate and all that?'

I said I did.

'I am not talking about all this fiddle with which side the white wine glass goes. We are not making a waiter of you. The basics.'

'I think I have those.'

Of course I knew how to use a flush. But what I had never used was a bath and didn't know that one had to rinse the fugitive hairs off its surface and wipe any possible scum from it or get into the deepest embarrassment with the landlady looking at you as though you had been rejected from the zoo. What I didn't know was that windows which opened to let in the fresh air had to be secured in their open positions by the metal strips with holes in them; else the wind could wrench them off their hinges and drop them in the garden, smashing the panes and infuriating that same dragon of a landlady who would proceed to punish your negligence and stupidity by having it repaired only six days later, leaving you to shiver with an open window in the winter cold. But all that came later.

The next day in Bombay I turned up for the tailor's appointment. The tailor awaited me in the boardroom. He had several bales and lengths of materials which his assistant had piled on the table. He had a tape measure slung around his neck, as much a part of his uniform as a stethoscope is a doctor's.

Mrs V swept into the room before me smoking a cigarette in a holder.

'You must choose some material for your Oxford bags and for a jacket.'

Why she issued that invitation I didn't know, because even as I was looking through the bales, she indicated three of them and said, 'He'll have a pair of trousers from each of these and this tweed for the jacket.'

'Very good choice madam has made,' the tailor said, all smiles. He took my measurements.

'And now the suit?'

So she was going to let me choose something. I went through the offered suit lengths and pulled one out.

'This one,' I said, failing in my attempt at assertiveness.

She frowned. She was not pleased.

'Mr Dhondy!' She threw the piece on the table. 'No gentleman wears a brown suit.'

I carried a grey suit with me to Britain.

SEVERING TIES

GOING ABROAD MEANT severing ties with very many things and people I knew and loved. The main wrench was leaving my teenage sweetheart behind.

Being in love with the general's daughter hadn't been easy. Mala's father's house was a large black stone affair called Flagstaff House. It was the official residence of the General Officer, Commanding in Chief, Southern Command. It was in the quiet part of the town, the leafy section of Poona Cantonment, and its gates were guarded by armed Gurkhas from the general's regiment. They would let in no one except recognized tradesmen and marked army cars. Young bearded men on bicycles stood no chance. The sentries in their boxes wouldn't even wander out to see who you were or what sort of enquiry you were making. They pretended you were invisible and inaudible and in fact did not exist in their scheme of things.

Occasionally, the Gurkha driver, one Eta Singh Gurung, who drove Mala to college in the family's white Ambassador car flying the general's black-and-red flag with stars, would recognize her friends and could vouch for us. He would step in if he happened to see us from within the compound and intercede. Then the gates would open and close behind us.

At first I only dared go when the general was away at the wars or wherever it was he went and then Mala would invite a few boisterous friends round to drink his whisky and play records on their primitive hi-fi. When he was away, the elder sister was in charge of the cooks and butlers and as she quite approved of me, she would ask us, me and other friends, to stay for dinner and get the cook to lay on the extra.

It was a formal house with crossed swords on the wall, high ceilings, carpets such as I hadn't seen before and a bewildering number of rooms, most of which were unused by this family of the general and his two daughters. Some nights Mala would sneak out of the house by the back gate, passing the sentries who were themselves anonymous and would have no means of conveying intelligence of this sort to the general, and we would go out of town on my borrowed motorcycle and talk and canoodle till dawn. Then she'd slip back in and pretend to have been there all night when her maid came to wake her. We'd meet on campus again later in the day.

I had had girlfriends before, but this one was different. Mala was remarkable in that unlike other sixteen- and seventeen-year-old girls one met, despite belonging to the highest echelons of Indian professional society, she was willing to throw its constraints completely aside. She seemed curious and wild and willing to go in the direction that her curiosity and wildness would take her. The absence of convention and of conventional shame and inhibition was refreshing. It was strikingly attractive. Apart from the slightly broad nose, she was very good-looking, tall, thin, with a provocative bob of black hair.

After the first few days of making her acquaintance and tacitly pairing up with her, the status of her being the general's daughter stopped being positive and became a drag. She'd be recognized, patronized and, when her father was around, subject, with the best of intentions, to the incubus of her chauffeur being sent everywhere with her and waiting around to drive her home.

I'd give her and another intimate friend of ours, formal lessons in logic, a subject on their Arts syllabus. Logic was not much more than the definitions and rules of deduction and induction. I would explain the texts, and then tea would be brought in a tray with the house china and we'd pretend we hadn't been there the day before, stealing the whisky and necking on the rug.

When I left for England we promised to write and thought that promising to stay faithful would be too bourgeois and corny.

ARTIES AND HEARTIES

THE LETTERS TO and from Mala became less frequent. Life in Cambridge was absorbing and offered all manner of challenges. Having produced a play for the Pembroke Players which was well reviewed in my first term, I was approached to join the University's dramatic society, the Amateur Dramatic Club, and was offered what they called a 'nursery production'. I was asked to a meeting of the committee and said I could adapt an Indian novel for the stage, but the committee which was accepting me as one of its novice directors insisted that it should be a play by a contemporary British playwright.

I researched these and decided to present them with something unusual – taking three of Harold Pinter's plays and turning them into an interwoven single presentation. They accepted and I set about casting, rehearsing and planning the set and the lighting, with other first-timers and a very limited budget.

The production took time away from my physics, chemistry, maths and crystallography studies in the evenings, but now the days seemed crowded with an absorbing purpose and new friends. One of them was Bill Thomas, a strapping Welshman who divided his time between rehearsing our play and rowing for his college. He had become quite famous as he was one of the few first-years who had been picked to row in the University team against Oxford in the annual Easter race. He confessed that it was a hard routine with early morning rowing practice throughout the winter and more training in the evenings.

As a fresher rowing for the University, he had been interviewed by *Varsity*, the University student newspaper and had his photograph on three pages of the issue.

He was reading Oriental languages and had chosen classical Sanskrit and Pali as his particular languages. He claimed to speak Sanskrit and had astounded the professor of classical Oriental languages when he began a conversation with him using what was deemed the correct pronunciation. He looked the most unlikely interpreter of ancient Indian texts, but that was probably what he would end up doing.

I'd given Bill a major role in one of the amalgamated plays. Cambridge was divided roughly into arties and hearties and I had no idea that Bill had been attending trials to be selected for the University boat crew. Like the rest of the cast and crew, when he auditioned and I offered him the part, he had sworn that the play would be his first commitment.

When it came to it, we had to adjust rehearsal times for his benefit; he was a born charmer and put the problem of the clash of his commitments to the cast and crew himself and won them over with very sincere-sounding regrets and offers to leave the play.

The cast and crew, including myself, fell for it. We would assemble and rehearse only after dinner each day as his rowing commitments were always at the crack of dawn and before sunset.

He was a handsome lad and girls who like their men big were attracted to him. He would boast that between rehearsing and training for the boat race, as well as attending lectures and tutorials, the only time he had for encountering his girlfriends was in the small hours of the morning. The boast generated a certain amount of scepticism until a girl called Ariadne began to wait for him each day through rehearsals and walked out arm in arm with him after.

Bill lived in the modern-architectured student block of Churchill College, which was, uniquely amongst the colleges, not walled to keep out undergraduates who hadn't made it through the gates by 10.30 p.m., extended on some days to midnight.

He spent a lot of time with his professor whom he had befriended. There was a very small band of scholars devoted to Sanskrit and Pali and it was predictable that their scholastic pursuits would bring about some camaraderie and socializing. Bill told us that Professor Heidt approved of his acting but very strongly disapproved of the rowing and rugby which he thought were superfluous activities at the University.

As Easter approached, the national newspapers carried stories about the Oxford and Cambridge boat crews. The race took place each year on the Thames and thousands of people gathered on the bridges and the accessible riverbanks to watch and cheer on their favourite eight. It was a national event much beloved of the betting shops and bookies.

Our performance of the plays took place at the end of term two weeks before the big race. On the day of the performance Bill turned up, in the nick of time, with his right arm in a sling and limping with a crutch under his armpit. He had had an accident but he swore he would be capable of acting his role. He was playing a tramp so it wouldn't matter if he had a sling. He could, he said, dirty the sling and tear it to make it look street-soiled and he had, he said, doctored his crutch to look decrepit.

He had left us no choice but to agree. There wasn't even time to ask him how he had acquired a broken arm and bruised leg. He told the other actors he'd tell them after the performance.

Ariadne wasn't at the performance, which went very well, with Bill limping on to stage for three curtain calls. After the performance, as we gathered round him, he would only say that he had had an accident and fallen out of the first floor window of his room on to the brick paving under it and broken his arm and hurt himself. Ariadne had left Cambridge since it was the end of term.

'How could you fall out of a window?' several people asked.

'I have been sworn to secrecy,' he said.

The secret emerged in the Easter holidays. The national papers carried the news that Bill Thomas had had a misadventure and had withdrawn from the Cambridge rowing eight. The Cambridge coach commented that he was furious as Thomas had no business to let the side down by courting injury in the way in which he had acquired it. The coach didn't elaborate.

Bill did. He wrote an exclusive for a national tabloid confessing that he and his girlfriend, who was Greek, had been caught having sex in his college rooms by the girl's narrow-minded father. The intruding father had attempted to drag the poor girlfriend away and this had led to a wrestling match between the father and Bill which had resulted in the latter being thrust out of the open window of his room.

'Bastard! He didn't want to be in the Cambridge boat at all. It was just a way of withdrawing at the last minute, causing a small hullabaloo and selling his story to the newspapers,' my neighbour Paul said.

'You mean he didn't fall out of the window?'

'Probably jumped and got bruised and made up the whole thing about the Greek father.'

When term began we had a reunion for cast and crew. Bill's arm and leg had healed. His college questioned him about the incident and, it was said, narrowly decided to overlook the alleged breach of the rules. No doubt Professor Heidt was reluctant to lose his best Sanskrit scholar – they weren't two-a-penny. It was rumoured that he was pleased that Bill wouldn't be distracted by rowing for the rest of his time at Cambridge.

'So it was all a farce?' I asked. 'Was Professor Heidt in on your plot? Insurance against being sent down?'

'Each man in his time plays many parts, some acts leading to newspaper wages,' he said.

A PASSAGE TO KING'S

A FRIEND AT King's told me that if we waited at a particular spot in the front quadrangle of King's College at a particular hour on Sunday evenings, we could observe E.M. Forster emerging from King's College chapel and crossing the quad to his rooms on the first staircase in the building opposite.

I, of course, wanted to set eyes on Forster, all or most of whose books I'd read. To Indians he was something of an icon having written two books about India – *The Hill of Devi*, a memoir of his days in the service of a maharaja, and A *Passage to India*, which had become a classic.

So my friend and I waited outside the chapel at the time he thought Forster was to be seen or encountered. I contemplated approaching him when he emerged. But what should one do? Ask him for his autograph? Approach him and say we were fans?

As we waited, I noticed that a group of people, three men in suits and raincoats and three or four women in saris, an obviously Indian crowd, had entered the quad and were standing by the entrance to the chapel. One of the men spoke to the usher or whoever it was in tail-coated uniform at its gates.

We could hear the choir singing. The Indian group moved away and seemed to wander off towards the Backs and the river, out of sight of the front quad. It was approaching summer and the light of day would last till past seven or even eight o'clock. The lights of the chapel were visible through its stained-glass windows.

We knew that the prayers and the sermon would end the service and then we'd see him. We did. The congregation at the Sunday service emerged and went their ways. We watched, surveying the faces. Foster emerged walking with his stick, accompanied by four or five people. The group blithely walked across the grass lawn of the quadrangle, a privilege unavailable to undergraduates, so they must have been senior members of the University or friends of Forster who were winging it.

In the circumstances we decided that having glimpsed him in person was all we would get that day as it would be inappropriate to interrupt the group who crossed the quad at the slow pace Forster set. We watched as he and his group reached the entrance to his staircase. They paused and spoke to him, presumably saying their goodbyes as all of them left and we saw a valet emerging to escort the old man in.

I looked at my friend. Should we be bold and walk up to him in the vestibule and say we just wanted to pay our respects? We moved towards where Forster was holding the valet's hand and crossing the vestibule. As if from nowhere, the group of seven Indian ladies and gentlemen appeared. They were carrying cameras and umbrellas and appeared to be tourists. They must have been watching from some hidden vantage and without any inhibition crowded round the entrance; as we got within earshot, I heard their spokesman say, 'Mr Forster, we have come all the way from India to admire you, sir.'

The greeting seemed to have succeeded in getting them invited in as they all disappeared, following Forster and his valet into the hallway and probably into his rooms. We had been too slow.

I did meet Forster, but only a few years after I had left the University. I was teaching a group of wayward boys, on a part-time assignment to earn some money, at a 'crammer' in a boarding house in a town called Market Harborough near Leicester, where I was doing a thesis on Rudyard Kipling.

The crammer was for boys who had, for one misdemeanour or another, been expelled from the more renowned public schools of Britain. So there were lads from Eton, Harrow, Rugby and Marlborough among others, who had been enrolled in the crammer, which was run by a gentleman and his wife. They owned this large house in the town and hired part-time tutors, graduate students such as myself, to coach the dropouts, mostly brilliant or at least academically very able lads, for their A-level exams.

Two of my pupils, to whom I was teaching among other books *A Passage to India*, were Phil and Nigel Havers. They were the sons of Sir Michael Havers, who was to be the law minister in Margaret Thatcher's government, but had been at the time the defence lawyer of The Rolling Stones who had been charged with drug offences. Nigel and Phil had no doubt got to meet the Stones through this connection and had been expelled from Rugby for smoking or possessing or spreading cannabis.

Nigel wanted me to take them to Cambridge, which I did. On a whim we knocked at Forster's door and were invited in. We exchanged polite compliments and left.

Very many years later, when Nigel had made a career as a successful actor on British TV, he wrote his autobiography. At one point he tells the story of our visit to Forster's rooms and goes on to say that the old man had put his hand on Nigel's thigh under the table. The pass had escaped me.

WRAP IT IN LEAD

THE THIRD TERM of the first year came to an end and we had our exam results. None of our acquaintances had spectacular results but none of them failed either.

The two notable academic failures of the year were Rajiv Gandhi, the future prime minister of India, and Taher Ayub, the dispenser of whisky, patron of the subcontinentals and son of the military dictator, the Martial Law Administrator Ayub Khan who had seized power in Pakistan. His departure seemed to mean an end to social contact at the University between Indians and Pakistanis.

There was always lively and sometimes hostile political debate in venues where we met, such as the Sidgwick Buttery where most Arts students had their lectures.

Partition was still a less-than-twenty-year memory. None of us, Indian or Pakistani students, were of a generation that had suffered the tragedy or slaughter of it. The Indians were certainly sceptical about Pakistan's stability, its suspension of democracy and the direction it had taken in allying itself with America.

Taher's salon had acted as a temptation with its ample supply of whiskies and vodkas in his cabinet, a luxury that no other undergraduates or even the dons could boast. On our last visit before the end of the term after which Taher was sent down, we had a sort of last supper. I was invited to his rooms with a few other Indians.

Taher and his chief lieutenants began to discuss which restaurant they should patronize that night. They decided on Varsity, one of the town's famous eateries, and after several drinks, we stepped out in a crowd. I still didn't know who would pay for the meal and was calculating that if I had to it would mean an overdraft of my entire next month's spending allowance.

We ordered our food and as we ate, one of the Pakistanis around the table, a fat young man with a reputation of being an Urdu poet, called quiet dignified attention to himself as his eyes welled up with tears which trickled down his cheeks.

Conversation stopped.

'What's wrong with him?' Taher asked in Urdu.

The poet didn't volunteer an answer. The young man sitting next to him did.

'Bet you he is crying because we are enjoying ourselves and he is thinking of the poor who have nothing to eat,' he said and laughed. The others laughed too. The poet remained straight-faced, the tears still dripping off his jowls.

It seemed to me they were motivated by a surfeit of whisky rather than any guilty or poetic sentiment about the starving masses.

Taher paid for the meal. I never met him again.

The one Pakistani whom I was to meet again and again was Akbar Ahmed. I used to meet him at Taher's soirées.

One day we were passing each other, cycling across Queen's College Bridge when he called out to me.

'Farrukh, you are at the ADC,' he said, 'and in the Pembroke Players, yaar? I have written a play. Will you read it and tell me what you think? I mean if you like it, you can direct it for me.'

'Sure, send it to me,' I said.

He did. The manuscript was delivered to me the next day. I read it but couldn't see, as the Master of Trinity said when turning down a popular applicant for the post of residential poet, 'any discernible merit in the work'. But I might have been wrong, mistaken, prejudiced. It was a saga, a political epic of sorts involving Pakistan's triumph over Indian treachery. Perhaps I was biased.

Ahmed accosted me a few days later.

'So what do you think?' I didn't want to say it was not to my taste so I thought of a dodge which would let me off that particular hook.

'Oh yeah, interesting. I've given it to the artistic committee of the Players and let's see what they say about adopting it as a production. There are of course a hundred plays being considered, classics to modern, you know.'

'Of course, of course. If they want to ask me questions or clarifications, that'll be fine,' he said.

I hadn't then given it to anyone but I thought it best to retrospectively give some truth to my lie, so I took the manuscript over to Donald, who was designated to be the next artistic director of the Players.

'You read all these submissions, so can you treat this as one?' I ventured. 'And will you talk to the writer about it?'

Donald took the manuscript, put it down and rubbed his hands in mock glee. 'I'd love to,' he said.

When I saw him in Hall at a distance two days later he knew what I was going to ask and he gestured with a downturned thumb and a frown which turned into a smile.

He said nothing to me then but the next day when I was hanging around the Sidgwick Buttery I saw him and before he'd said anything to me as we sat down to a coffee together, Ahmed spotted us and came up.

'Did you get...' he started, but before he could finish I introduced them. This was my way out.

'Sure. This is Donald, he's read your play and...'

'Great, great,' Ahmed said and he pulled a stool and sat down. 'I know it's not perfect but you guys are experienced and you can tell me what it needs.'

'I'll tell you what it needs. Are you sure you can take this?' Donald said.

'Sure, sure, anything,' Ahmed said, anxiously, shifting his ample weight on the tiny stool.

'What it needs is lead.'

'Lead?'

'Yeah. Buy a sheet of lead, wrap the manuscript of your play in it, and throw it into the Cam,' Donald said.

It took a while for the severity to hit Ahmed. His puzzlement turned to clear understanding.

'Ah,' he said. 'Ah, you didn't like it. Okay, okay, okay. That's fine, but can you return the manuscript?'

'I'll get it to you,' I said. I felt a bit sorry for him. There was no need for Donald to have put it quite that way.

Ahmed went out of the Buttery and returned a minute later. He grinned and leaned over our table addressing Donald.

'That was a humorous way of rejection. It needs lead! I won't forget that,' he said and, still grinning, walked out.

'A character. You should cast him in a production,' Donald said.

Decades later, I met Akbar Ahmed in different circumstances. By this time he was a professor of Islamic studies at Selwyn College, Cambridge, having induced some rich Islamic foundation to fund such a seat which he could fill. He and my friend, the film director Jamil Dehlavi, approached me to write the screenplay for a film on the founder of Pakistan, Muhammad Ali Jinnah, which I did and which Ahmed didn't ask me to wrap in lead and throw in the Thames or the Indus. The two of them produced my screenplay.

ON THE ROAD

THE SUMMER HOLIDAYS were upon us and Johnny and I decided that we would hitch rides through Europe and Asia to India, to Bombay and then, by train of course, to Jamshedpur where my parents were. My geography was not too reliable, but Johnny had worked out the route more or less, planning to stick to the main highways connecting the country.

We'd hitch to Dover and take the ferry to Calais – for which we'd have to buy a ticket. Then we'd travel through Belgium to Germany and south through Austria to Yugoslavia, Bulgaria and Turkey. We'd go from Istanbul to Ankara and thence over the mountains to Iran and through Tehran to Meshed and the Afghan coast.

Carrying an Indian passport, I wouldn't be allowed to pass through Pakistan so we would get to Afghanistan and then perhaps pay for a flight to Delhi. The alternative would be to work our way to the Persian Gulf port city of Quaramshar or Abadan and then try to get a cheap trip across the Arabian Sea to an Indian port.

It was an ambitious plan and we thought we'd make it within four or five or at the most six weeks, leaving us another six in India, after which we would buy single plane tickets to get back to London and Cambridge. Johnny said he had a savings account he could raid and I knew that I had an old motorcycle which my uncle had given me lying on a veranda in Poona and I could sell that and pay for my fare back.

We set out from the University and landed in London. I was sleeping on the floor of the tiny rented bedsitter belonging to my poet friend Adil Jussawalla. Those were days when the Victorian terraces of South Kensington were divided into a warren of bedsits by largely unscrupulous landlords. The rooms were tiny, with the floor space of two or three single beds.

We spent a few nights in London gathering visas for the different countries we'd pass through. In the evenings, after the visa offices had shut, Johnny would go back to his sister's flat in Swiss Cottage and Adil and I would nip out of the depressingly tiny space of his room to the corner pub.

After the fourth night, waking up in Adil's room with the calculation that there was only the Iranian visa to go, I felt a sharp pain in my throat.

'Oh my God, what's happened to your neck,' Adil said, brewing up the morning tea.

'Throat hurts like hell.'

'Your neck's swollen. Go to the shower room where there's a mirror.'

I looked in the mirror. It was as though I was wearing a thick skin-coloured collar. I couldn't even swallow the tea.

I wasn't registered with a doctor but I could, Adil said, go to the nearest hospital accident and emergency wing. I did.

'Mumps,' the doctor said after a few seconds of examining me. 'Where are you living and with whom?'

I explained my circumstances.

'Isolation ward for you, young man,' he said.

I took a bus to the hospital in West Brompton where they said they had a bed for me. Adil would phone Johnny and tell him that our trip would have to wait for ten days as the doctors said there was no cure, it was a waiting game and if I wasn't careful it would affect my testicles and render me permanently impotent.

The only question of potency that had ever occurred to me was having some form of contraception during my initiation into sex. The idea of having children at some time, however remote, struck me for the first time. Doctors came to my isolation cubicle every day and felt my testicles for swellings or whatever. They didn't explain. I was confined to a glass cabin with a radio on the bedside table and a copy of *In Cold Blood* by Truman Capote which Adil had lent me.

Adil brought me clothes and comfort. Johnny came but said he hadn't had mumps so was enjoined to stay outside the booth and not visit too often for fear of catching the virus. Apart from the nurses who looked after me, the only other person who came into my cabin was the lady with the metal tea trolley. She was Spanish and didn't speak much English.

She would push the trolley in with a smile saying: 'Cup-o-tea, cup-o-tea...'

'Ah, you mean Truman Capote?' I said one day.

'What is Truman?'

'Truman is Capote,' I said and showed her the cover of the book I was holding.

That evening the duty nurse in charge of the ward walked in.

'What have you been telling Invicta?'

'We just chat, not even small talk, minute talk!'

'Did you tell her not to say cup of tea?'

'What do you mean? Of course not.'

'She's been going round the ward saying "tru-man, tru-man", and the patients are bewildered. When I asked her she said you told her to say it instead of offering the ward tea.'

I explained and pleaded unwitting innocence but she, smiling with a twist to the corners of her lips, left unconvinced.

Though the illness had left me feeling feeble and we had lost ten days of our possible sojourn in India, eventually we set out.

Johnny said we were not hitching after we hit Austria. He had discovered a chain of public bus and coach trips which would take us from Salzburg, through Yugoslavia, Bulgaria and Turkey and deposit us in Tehran. He had bought two sets of tickets for the succession of carriers but they were for specific dates so no more mumps or prevarication. We had to get to Salzburg on the start date.

I was afraid of travel sickness, the constant bane of my youth – malodorous or stuffy cars whose drivers give two male travellers a lift, the channel crossing and then perhaps coaches whose windows don't open and, the ultimate dread, the stink of other passengers with the same affliction.

We carried what we called army-surplus haversacks on our backs with nylon sleeping bags, a few clothes, a small gas stove to boil packet soups on the way and our toothbrushes. Johnny is a gaunt six foot with spindle shanks and his ribs prominent through the skin of his chest. His teeth were stained yellow through smoking twenty a day.

We got to Dover in a few hours in a friendly truck and the trucker offered to take us across the channel as part of his crew, so we could save the ferry fare. By the first night we were on the outskirts of Brussels and were invited by the Belgian driver of another truck that was on its way to Germany to sleep in the back. It was the hospitality of the road and fuelled us with optimism for the journey.

In Munich, we slept in a park and cooked soup for our supper in the single pan that Johnny carried strapped to the outside of his haversack. In the middle of the night we woke up with police torches in our faces. We were ordered to get up and gather our things, then taken to a police station and locked in a cell. We were asked to hand over our passports. I knew a smattering of German, perhaps enough to ask why we had been arrested but not enough to understand the answer.

By the middle of the morning they returned our passports and let us out of the station. The officer who released us indicated by gestures that we were to move on, out of the city and never to dent the grass of the parks of their fair city again. We nodded and thanked him, enquired our way to the highway and set off for Salzburg.

A moustachioed German man in a brown suit, driving a large Mercedes, stopped for us. He was very proud of his accented English and said he only stopped because he spotted Johnny and knew from the hanging saucepan that he was an Englishman. He thought this was a hilarious observation and repeated it several times.

After several kilometres he drove off the Autobahn.

'I must to you something show,' he said.

In about twenty minutes we passed through a village and came to a small hillock where he parked.

'We have to get to Salzburg by this evening. By six o'clock if possible, we have a night coach to catch,' Johnny protested.

'You have not worries. You must see history first. I am charging,' Moustachio said.

He wasn't charging. He meant he was in charge. He asked us to follow him out of the car and on to a path on the hillock. We walked a hundred yards and there was a cement structure built into the hillside.

'Is top secret. Hitler in Berlin didn't commit suicide as everybody in history is believing. But is not right. He was dying in this boonker, just here. See it?'

'How do you know that? Why doesn't anyone else?'

'My father was a Nazi,' he said, 'and he was with Hitler in the boonker and put fire to his body here on the hillside. You can big holes from British bombs see. I will show.'

'No, no, we better go,' Johnny said.

Moustachio shrugged. He'd shown us essentially what he wanted to and so we set off again in the Merc; true to his word, he got us to the coach station a few minutes before six when boarding for Zagreb began.

We drove in the coach through the night, Johnny assuring me that he had booked this specific ride so we wouldn't have to pay for a bed or sleep rough in a park, in a bus shelter or under a bridge. After a succession of coaches for two days, we arrived in Istanbul. It was the first city in our schedule in which we had a few days to be tourists. We saw the sights.

We found a cheap hostel which advertised itself in Turkish as a 'hotel for workers'. It was cheaper than the youth hostels we had found so we paid a deposit and were instructed to get there just before ten o'clock as they wouldn't admit anyone after that time.

We arrived at ten and were shown into a dormitory with perhaps forty beds in it. We had to stow our luggage under the beds and in fifteen minutes the lights, all but the blue night-light, were turned off.

At precisely six in the morning an attendant shook me awake. At the foot of the bed, the next occupant for the day shift was waiting. The attendant indicated that my tenure of the bed was over and I should get my luggage and clear off. The next occupant, a tall Turkish man who looked from the mud on his clothes and hands like a building site labourer, looked me up and down as I attempted to change my shirt by the side of the bed. He was impatient to climb into the bed. As I got my rucksack from under it and loaded it on to my back Johnny came up from his bed further down the room. My successor tenant, now on his back with the blanket pulled up to his neck, saw him and gave us a deep disapproving look. The likes of me, with my changes of shirt, portable wardrobe and blonde companion shouldn't have been availing of this cheap resting place.

We got a coffee and went back to the dosshouse at which we had spent the previous night to book another, but were told that they were full. No room at that inn!

Three days later we crossed the Bosphorus on a ferry into Asia.

◆

The youth hostel in Ankara was a renovated shabby 'hotel', full that night of American youths. There was a dining room in which the evening meal, included in the bed-and-board deal, was served. It had one very long antique table with benches on all four sides to seat perhaps sixteen guests.

As we sat down to the meal with the Americans referring to the served kebabs as 'dick-burgers', two well-groomed young men in summer suits came in with a man of uncertain age with long, ginger, matted hair, an overgrown beard which wisped down towards his chest, wearing a very new Turkish shirt and obviously new but ill-fitting flared trousers. He would have fitted in with the scruffy travellers in the hostel but the two young men, who looked like his captors or like plainclothes policemen in charge of him in some way, were out of place.

As our attention was drawn to their entry, one of the captors addressing the dining company asked, 'Any Brits here?'

'Yes, what is it?' Johnny said.

'Where are you from and what are you doing in Ankara?'

'What the fuck is that to do with you?' Johnny said, genuinely incredulous.

'Hold on, hold on. I am sorry if we seemed in a hurry,' the other young man said. He approached Johnny and held out his hand. 'I am Graves, from the British embassy. That's Johnson. We need a favour. Patriotic favour, that's why this question.' He looked around the curious and silent gathering.

'Any other Brits?'

'Farrukh's Indian but we're undergrads – Cambridge – travelling to India.'

Graves extended his hand to me.

'That's exactly appropriate,' he said to Johnny. 'Can we have a word with you?'

Johnny stepped out of the bench and walked some distance with Graves, returning a few minutes later. The ginger-bearded man stood with his head down, absolutely still, next to Johnson, who was surveying the faces in the room. Johnny put his hand gently on the shoulder of the ginger beard.

'I am John Snow,' he said, softly.

'This is Ivan McIllwraith,' Johnson said. 'You hungry, Ivan? It's dinner being served.'

Ivan didn't answer and Johnny sat him down between us on the bench.

The proprietor, now acting as waiter, put a plate of food down in front of Ivan who grabbed at it as a starving man might. He rammed it down his throat. Graves and Johnson looked satisfied. They nodded to Johnny and left. Ivan eyed my plate which still had half a circle of Turkish pide, the bread, and some yogurt salad on it.

'You can have that, I'm done,' I said, though I wasn't quite.

He grabbed my plate and the food was soon gone. Johnny negotiated another chunk of bread and some stuff for Ivan.

'We're here for a couple of days with you,' he said to Ivan. 'Graves said they have to clear some official stuff but they'll get you back to Scotland maybe even tomorrow or the day after.'

Ivan now put his arm on Johnny's shoulder for a brief moment. Then he turned to me and did the same, wordlessly. A tear trickled down his cheek.

At that moment the lights went out and the room was plunged into darkness. The five or six Americans at the table whooped.

'Power cut, jeez!' one of them shouted. 'Them Turks ain't got the energy act together.'

The proprietor and his wife and daughter came in with candles and placed them on the table and around the room.

In that dim light, Ivan, prompted by Johnny, hesitatingly, in slow sentences, told his story. He was from the north of Scotland and an archaeology student. He had come to Turkey three years ago on an archaeological dig with a professor and three other students. He had a dispute with one of the students, a girl, and had left the group and gone into the mountains outside Ankara on his own. When he mentioned the three years, his voice broke.

A gang of people he called Turkish gypsies encountered him camping in the mountains and seeing he was alone, kidnapped him, chained him with a lock around his neck and wrists and enslaved him. He was made to do the dirty work of their itinerant camp, tending to the donkeys, carrying the camp equipment as they shifted from one place to another, fetching water from the streams in the rocks and valleys with his legs chained together and to his hands to prevent his escape. He tried escaping a couple of times but was easily captured, brought back to camp and beaten senseless for the attempt.

A few days ago he managed to escape under cover of darkness when the entire camp, after a celebration of some gypsy festival, was drunk and his jailor had neglected to chain him to the circular stone which was his anchor at night and which he had to carry from camp to camp.

'Three years of my...' he said and a sob escaped him. No one interrupted him. There was complete, overawed silence in the candlelit room.

'Three years of my life, just gone,' he said; we could hear him fighting back a choking sob.

Then from the end of the table the young American with the baseball cap turned on its side slapped his thigh and said, 'Yeah man! Gotta watch them gypsies!'

◆

The mountains between Turkey and Iran were barren and bleak and the road through them winding and precarious. The coaches we had ridden in up to Ankara were now replaced by rickety buses with, I supposed, hardy enough engines to tackle the slopes. I was sick all through the seemingly never-ending twists and turns and the horror of others being just as sick made it worse.

We spent one night in a bus shelter in Erzerum and were off the next day. The language changed, the currency changed, our passports were diligently checked. Each time that was done, the officials separated me from the Iranian, British and Turkish passport holders. I was, for some reason, suspect and was carried away for questioning, which was futile as I didn't know any Farsi and my questioners didn't know any English. They had to satisfy themselves with endlessly and meaninglessly turning the pages of my passport before handing it back to me and escorting me to the bus in which the other passengers were being held up till I returned; the passengers were not shy in demonstrating their resentment – a jeer and a lot of jabbering filled the bus as I was escorted on to it and one of them even spat into the aisle as I passed.

In Tehran we had heard that the Sikh temple, the gurdwara, allowed travellers such as ourselves to camp in their humble courtyard. We had been told that they would even feed you a free meal a day. It turned out to be true. I spoke to the granthi, the keeper of the temple, in Hindi, which endeared us to him and whereas the other travellers, three or four of them, were assigned the verandas that ran like humble cloisters round three sides of a courtyard with several rooms off them, we were assigned a very sparse room with two jute-strung cots. After the hard soil of the parks and the floors of bus shelters in which we'd slept, this was a luxury and so was the exposed tap in the courtyard under which we could squat to have a bath.

The granthi wore Punjabi pyjamas and a long shirt which covered his knees and he had a white beard down to his chest. I suspect he hid some baldness inside his turban. He had laughing eyes which widened and narrowed in a fascinating puppet show of interest and emotion as he questioned us in detail about who we were, our families, our travel, our studies, our ambitions and the state of our finances. He said the meal would be delivered that evening by the women of Tehran's Sikh community who cooked communally and fed him and the travellers passing through. They did. We ate daal and brinjals and naan.

One of the travellers sleeping on the veranda in rolled blankets was, he told us over the communal meal, bicycling to Europe from India. He had crossed the Himalayas and the Afghan plateaus on his bike and here he was in Tehran. In a few days he would set out for Turkey, going by bike the way we had come in buses.

We asked him why he was travelling by bike. Wouldn't the cost of his living during the slow journey exceed the fare we were paying for buses? It's possible he didn't understand the question or maybe he did because he said, 'I am loving cycling.'

He unbelted and lowered his trousers to his ankles, intent

on showing his right knee to the assembly of four travellers and the granthi.

'No patella,' he said.

He invited us in turn to touch his knee and ascertain for ourselves that his right knee lacked a kneecap. Johnny asked him how he'd lost it. I translated. He said he was born without one and that's the reason he had taken to cycling. It must have made sense.

After two days at the gurdwara the cyclist left, his blankets and belongings tied behind him, on his journey to Europe. I had asked him which bit of Europe he was bound for and what he would do there. He said he had heard that Bulgaria was the most hospitable and he would probably stay there before trying to get to England and hand in his personal petition to the Queen to abolish all forms of motor transport and get the world cycling again. It was the only hint he gave anyone of his real abolitionist mission.

As he went, his last word to me was that my English companion and I should abjure all contact with motorized transport and walk to India if we couldn't afford bicycles.

◆

We were preparing to leave the next morning when into the gurdwara courtyard came two very weary travellers. Bruno was French and spoke very little English. He was round-faced, blonde and stocky, with stained brown and black teeth which didn't detract from the charm of his winning smile. Désirée was Dutch and as a consequence spoke English fluently but had lived in France for several years. She was tall and thin with a long face which could have been used as a model for Modigliani. She had long dark hair and long thin legs under her very travelled skirt and she wore huge tough ramblers' shoes which gave her legs the appearance of Olive Oyl, the heroine of the Popeye cartoons.

They put their packs down and sat in the courtyard. We were squatting outside our room and smoking cigarettes when Désirée approached us. She asked us what the procedure for getting a bed and a bath was. We said the granthi would emerge at some point and tell them where they could sleep and I pointed to the tap in the corner of the courtyard which served as the communal bathroom.

'I haven't had a bath for a month,' she said. She went and reported our conversation to Bruno and then walked to the tap with a cake of soap. She didn't take her shirt or skirt off as she was aware that apart from us there were three Sikhs huddled in the courtyard who could watch her at her ablutions. She squatted under the tap and the water cascaded down her hair which she soaped to a lather. She put her hand under her shirt and soaped herself. The shirt was now soaking wet and completely transparent so that one could see her nipples, boyish breasts and prominent ribs. The Sikhs, all old men, began to stare and they exchanged glances when she put her hand under her skirt to soap herself.

They said nothing, until Bruno approached the tap where she was bathing, having stripped and left his clothes in a pile on their backpacks. Then one of the Sikhs shouted in Farsi and then in English.

'No allow, no allow, towel, towel, towel.'

Bruno ignored them and went to the tap and moving Désirée aside squatted under it, his genitals showing.

The Sikhs, all three, stood up, and one pulled a small dagger from his waist. He started walking towards Bruno.

I grabbed my shirt which I had left drying on the veranda floor and ran to Bruno.

'Get out and wrap yourself,' I shouted.

Désirée saw the Sikh coming towards them with determined strides with his little dagger and she screamed.

'Shut up, no need for that,' I said.

Bruno got out from under the tap, grabbed the towel and wrapped it around his waist. He was grinning. Désirée was standing with her transparent shirt with her hand to her mouth, wide-eyed with suppressed screams.

'They will behave, Sardarji,' I said in Hindi.

'What do these bastard whites think?' he replied, brandishing his dagger. 'This is a gurdwara, not a brothel.'

'They don't know. They've been on the road for a month. Please.'

He put his dagger back in the scabbard under his long shirt and with a grunt of contempt turned back to his companions.

That night, around naan and kebabs which we bought in the side streets around the gurdwara, Bruno and Désirée told us that they were on a similar hitching trip to India. They had reached Meshed, the Iranian town on the border of Afghanistan, but found the border closed as there was plague in that part of Afghanistan and the Iranian government had sealed the borders. No one could cross and even if they could, why would they want to when it was reported that a sizeable portion of the population had succumbed to the bubonic plague.

The next day Johnny went to the British embassy and was told there that the current medical advice was that the borders to Afghanistan would remain closed for months. We discussed the alternatives to being trapped in or turning back from Iran. There was a land route across Pakistan via the Makran coast to the south or one could go to the coast and try and get a cheap voyage on a boat. I told them I couldn't get a visa to travel through Pakistan.

In all our time together in Tehran and later, journeying south to the seaports, Désirée would act as interpreter. Bruno was very effusive in French and would clench his fists and fly into a rage if we carried on a conversation for any prolonged length of time in English.

'Fuck you, fuck you! *Je m'en fou!*' he would shout and Johnny and I would break into,

'Frere Jacque, Frere Jacque,
Dormez vous, dormez vous?
Sonnez la matine...'

This would enrage him further but he would literally grin and bear it.

We got down to Quaramshar and to the fishing port. It took a few hours of enquiring but we were told that no cargo boats or any other craft travelled all the way to India. The Arabian Sea crossing was dangerous for small craft and only big ships left the larger ports for Surat and Bombay and points further south on the Indian coast. We were told they wouldn't take passengers.

While we were making these enquiries and finding a fisherman's dosshouse in which to sleep, we were approached by a squad of six policemen. They made it clear they wanted to see our passports. We complied. They looked through the passports, and returned all except mine. The officer holding my passport kept turning its pages, contributing to my anxiety. What was he looking for? Finally, after a couple of minutes, he signalled to his juniors who stepped forward and grabbed me by the shoulder. 'We're arresting you,' he said.

Johnny, Désirée and Bruno protested. It was the first time in my life I had been handcuffed. The policemen led me away to the gates of the port and shoved me in a van. My protests in English fell on deaf Iranian ears. Three armed policemen stood between me and my companions as two others escorted me away.

'I'll get to the British consulate,' Johnny shouted.

'Or the Indian,' I shouted back.

The police van took us to the town's police station and they threw me roughly into a cell, releasing my wrists from the handcuffs.

In an hour or so a policeman came in to see me.

'You are an Indian?' he said in broken Hindi pronounced in an Arabic accent.

'Yes, you people have got my passport.'

'It is not real passport. It is circus passport. You are Egyptian spy!' He was testing my ability with the language.

'Please don't be absurd,' I said in Hindi. 'I have never even been to Egypt. I am an Indian and I live at present in Britain.'

'We know you and we know why you have come,' he said ominously and turned his back on me; he was let out of my cell by the jailor.

I spent the night in the cell. I lay down on the wooden bunk but couldn't sleep. In the morning two Indian gentlemen were brought to the cell by the officer in charge, who handed me back my passport. One of the Indians looked at me curiously.

'Farrukh? Zareen's brother?' he asked.

'Yes,' I said.

'Don't you remember me? Jumpy Irani from your college in Poona.'

'Of course I do,' I lied.

'We are both consulate officials; we've come to release you,' he said. Then he said, turning to the other official, 'We were all in love with his sister, you know. She was so beautiful.'

Johnny, Bruno and Désirée were waiting for me outside the police station. Johnny had found that there was no British consulate in the town but had chanced upon an Indian travel office and they had contacted Jumpy and his colleague. It was all a mistake. The police here had to be wary of Egyptian infiltration.

I explained to Jumpy what we were doing there.

'No boats,' he said. 'They will take you on board and slit your throats.'

But he had an idea.

'I can drive you to the airport at Abadan and get you on a false diplomatic ticket on tonight's Air India flight to Bombay.'

If I had heard such good news before I couldn't remember when. But, of course, he could only pull it off for me and not for the other three. He could, however, help them to get to the Pakistan border quite easily.

I took the plane on the ticket Jumpy Irani fixed for me.

'Is your sister married?' he asked.

'Yes, very much and very happy,' I said.

He looked philosophical. 'I am also,' he said. 'You might remember Khursheed Khodadad? She was junior to us, but nowhere as beautiful as your sister Zareen.'

'What does beauty matter?' I said. 'As long as you love her.'

'Of course, of course I love her,' Jumpy said.

NEVER FOREVER

I LANDED IN Bombay the same night and made my way to my uncle's flat on Malabar Hill. He was surprised to see me.

'You were in England!'

'Holidays,' I said.

'Have you come all the way to see Mala?' he asked.

'Of course, but only if she wants to see me.'

'She came to lunch last Saturday and talked about nothing but you,' he said.

He told me that Mala had moved into a students' hostel for women on Marine Drive.

I had a shower, borrowed his car and drove down to find her.

I hadn't written to her for weeks and hadn't indicated to her that I was coming to India. I was asked by the receptionist to wait in the hall while she was summoned. She was told she had a guest, a young man.

I didn't expect her to look horrified at the sight of me, but she was and then she hugged me as I held her and started to cry.

'What are you doing? What about Cambridge? How did you... why...?'

There were too many questions and I led her out saying we'd drive out to a quiet beach and I'd tell her everything.

We drove north to a deserted beach with mangrove scrub and thorns in the sand. I parked with a view of the sea and I told her how I'd got there and that friends would join me as soon as they could get across Pakistan and down to Bombay.

'I want to go back with you to England,' she said.

Sitting in the front seats of the car we kissed, holding on to each other long and deep when there was the tapping of a wooden baton on the car window. A policeman in khaki uniform on a bicycle was tapping to get my attention. I rolled the window down.

'I am arresting you for immoral actions,' he said in Marathi.

'What immoral actions?' I demanded.

'You are bringing these prostitutes here...' I didn't let him finish. I got out of the car and confronted him.

'If you say that about my wife I will strangle you. I'm taking your number. You know who she is? She is the chief of the Indian army's daughter and I'm going to report you to the Commissioner of Police, you filthy dog.'

'Okay, okay, I go,' he said in English.

I watched him as he pedalled away a few feet. Then he stopped. He got off the bike and wheeled it back.

'I am sorry, sir,' he said. 'You see, we expect some little gift from people who come here to do these things. Not people like you, but bad people. Please, no complaint.'

I felt sorry for him.

'No complaint,' I reassured him and took a ten-rupee note out of my pocket and gave it to him.

'Keep the beaches moral,' I said.

He said 'thank you' and smiled and went his way.

Mala spent the night and the following night and the one following that with me. That first night, at my uncle's, she asked me if she could use the phone in private and she must have spent half an hour in my uncle's office on the phone. I could hear her raise her voice occasionally through the glass doors that separated the 'office' space – open to the sea-facing air on a veranda on the fifth floor of the block of flats – from the sitting room.

When she emerged she said she had to make excuses for not being in the hostel that night as the matrons would get alarmed and start calling her mother and perhaps even the police, saying she was missing.

I didn't ask what excuse she had given them or anyone else. I determined not to tell her about Enid and not to ask her how she had interpreted or acted upon our tryst of freedom. That night we knew we were in love again.

◆

A week after I got to Bombay, Johnny, Désirée and Bruno turned up, dusty, tired and hungry. My uncle's flat couldn't accommodate them for more than one night in the spare room that I was using – Bombay flats are notoriously small – but he got them rooms at his Western India Automobile Association Club.

The hostel did report Mala to her mother as they didn't believe the excuses she had given for being away for the whole week. Fortunately, my uncle, knowing her mother, had urged Mala to at least phone her and tell her where she was and assure her that she was safe. Her mother didn't approve of her being with me so my aunt had to get on the phone and assure Mala's mother that she would act as a responsible chaperone. Her responsibility stretched to telling my uncle to ensure that we used contraception when sleeping in their spare room.

Every time we made love, I thought of Enid's diaphragm. Were they available in India? I felt very self-conscious buying packs of condoms which, in the interest of birth control the government had encouraged every grocery store and chemist to sell. I looked around furtively for any packaging on and about the shelves displaying condoms which might contain diaphragms. I didn't see them; even if I had, I wouldn't have known how to introduce the idea of using one to Mala.

◆

A few days after they arrived in Bombay, Bruno and Désirée returned to my uncle's house wearing saffron robes and plastic slippers, their heads shaved. Désirée announced their conversion to Hinduism with a big grin. They were going to take a train to Benares that night and wash away their sins in the Ganges.

'You'll catch some awful disease,' my uncle said. 'There are dead bodies floating about of the desperately poor people who've died of some sickness and couldn't afford wood for cremation.'

Mala decided that she had to spend some time in her mother's flat and she would do that when I visited my aunts in Poona. Johnny accompanied me. When we returned to Bombay, we were both invited to Mala's mother's party. Mala said her school friend Fancy would be there. I had heard endlessly about this girl who had been a childhood friend of Mala's; her father was a diplomat and since she travelled with her parents all over the world, we had never met.

Her real name, as Mala had explained, was Fantasia, which was a name her mother had chosen on a whim. She was born in Vienna when her father was the Indian ambassador there and they had been to a concert the night before she was born and the mother had fallen in love with Schubert's Fantasia in F Minor, a duet for piano. Her father hadn't dissented when the mother started calling her newborn Fantasia and the name was soon officially adopted.

It must have been that 'Fantasia Moti Singh' sounded a bit exotic so when they returned to India her father started calling her Fancy and passed it off as a pet diminutive for some elaborate Sanskrit or Urdu name, such as Phenabhyam or Farzana, which she might have been christened with.

I met her parents too and the other guests who were introduced as general somebody and his wife. The general was a tall, handsome man who had lost one eye fighting wars on the Pakistan border. He was, we were told, a decorated hero. His wife had startlingly light brown hair, the colour of a cat's. Both Johnny and I agreed over a gin and lime cordial that she dyed her hair but Fancy put us right, saying that her mother was a German Jewess and she had inherited some of the blonde pigment from her.

Fancy stayed the night at Mala's mother's and the next morning on the pretext of going for a picnic Johnny and I picked them both up in my aunt's rickety old Fiat and we went to the British consulate. Mala wanted Fancy's moral support as we were going to enquire how she could get a visa to enter the UK.

We had argued over it, standing on the balcony, even as the party was in full swing.

'I want to go back with you. I'll work there, in Cambridge, in London. You said your friend Adil walked dogs and cleaned house. I can do that. I want to be with you forever. I can see now from your body language that you don't want me to. You're such a coward. You probably have some white girlfriend there. I am beginning to hate you,' she said.

'Don't be silly. I think they can hear you.'

'I don't care. About anything if...'

'Listen, just keep it down. Of course I want you to come. And no, I don't have what you call a girlfriend there. But how can you just come?'

'Why don't you find out?' she asked.

The person we spoke to at the consulate was sympathetic but said that Mala could only get a tourist visa and she would have to return after an allocated number of weeks. Of course if she was admitted to a registered university she could get a visa for the duration.

'What if we got married?' she asked.

'Well, you couldn't automatically get a visa if you were married to an undergraduate with an Indian passport. You'd have to marry someone with a UK passport and then you could apply for a British passport.'

'It's obvious,' Fancy interrupted. 'Why don't you marry Johnny and get a UK passport and go?'

'Why would Johnny marry me?'

'I don't care,' Johnny said. 'If that'll work I'll do it.'

'But you'll be married to him,' I said.

'They can get divorced,' Fancy said. 'And then she's all yours.'

'I bet this is the weirdest proposal anyone's ever had,' Mala said.

We discussed the idea into the night. Johnny called it a 'caper' and said he would do it for friendship as Sidney Carton had in *A Tale of Two Cities*.

'It's hardly the same thing,' I said. 'Chopping your head off would be more painful... I don't mean it'll be painful marrying Mala...'

'But you said it,' Mala said.

'I meant it will be like not marrying you, if you see what I mean.'

'How do you get married in India?'

'You go to the court or the registrar or something, don't you?'

'I don't want to shave my head,' Mala said.

We pointed out that she was already a Hindu, but Johnny might have to convert and shave his if he was getting married as one.

The discussion was light-hearted but I know that all of us

knew that it would be taking a serious step into the defiant unknown. Our families wouldn't approve. We'd have to leave Mala with the secret until she got her UK passport, we'd have to find the money for her ticket and how would we manage once she was in England? My stomach was in a tight knot as we discussed phoning my aunts to hand over my motorcycle to a friend who had said he was eager to buy it and he had ways of sending the money to Bombay.

The next day, with Fancy and me as witnesses, Johnny and Mala were married through Hindu ritual and given a certificate which the priest, who offered a discount if the converts or marrying couples paid in dollars or pounds, said was a legal document.

The only person in whom I confided was my uncle. He looked very worried. All he said was, 'There should have been another straightforward way. But now you've done it. If her mother asks me later even, I'll have to say you told me and that will put me in an awkward position. I won't lie.'

'I am sorry,' I said and the knot in my stomach added a tightening twist.

The next day I heard Mala on the phone say she had been invited with Fancy to my aunt's house in Poona and she had accepted the invitation because she could see her dad while she was there.

'Have you asked if he's in Poona?' her mother asked. 'I think he's in Delhi.'

'I spoke to his housekeeper and she said he may be back, so I'll take a chance,' Mala said. 'Can you tell Aunty Chopra that Fancy is with me and I shall be away for two days. She's got her clothes. I told her to call her mother herself, but you know how scatty she is and we've got to catch this train.'

'Are those boys going with you?' her mother asked.

'Of course they are coming. You know I know his aunts from last year in college there. Fancy says she's never been to Poona so I can show her my old college and the sights.'

'There aren't many sights in Poona,' her mother said. 'As long as you girls stay together and look after each other.'

'Sure Mummy, bye.'

She put the phone down. I was standing next to her.

'But you're, we're ... not going anywhere.'

'I had to do it for Fancy.'

'What do you mean do it for her, do what?'

'She's going away for two days and asked me to tell her mum that she was going in a gang with me and you.'

'But that's a lie!'

'Ah, you've become Jesus Christ, have you? Of course it's a lie, or as you said about our little plot, it's a strategy.'

'What's it for, where is she going?'

'A secret! You don't want to know.'

'I do,' I said.

'You know the general,' she said.

'Who? Cyclops? The one-eyed guy?'

'Have some respect,' she said even though she grinned. 'He lost his eye fighting for our country.'

'What about him?'

'Well, they are in love and he's taking her away for a couple of days so we are covering for her.'

'For God's sake, she is eighteen and he must be what, fifty-five?'

'He bought her a gold bracelet.'

'For God's sake, he's a friend of her father and mother.'

'I know,' Mala said. 'I told her it was very odd. He started it when he knew that she had a kind of girly crush on him.'

'So what happens if straw-head finds out? His wife?'

'How would she? The old mountain fox has covered their trail so far.'

'Wow! Does Fancy know that you're telling me all this?'

'She'll guess I guess. When Cyclops – we'll call him that, it's a good code name – asked her how she would get away she said the first thing that came into her head. She said she's told them that she's on a study trip to an archaeological site with a woman professor. Then of course she realised that's not what she can say because her father would definitely ask the professor how the trip went and what they found at the dig and all this rubbish. He is interested in archaeology. So I said I'd tell her parents she was with us. But Fancy told Cyclops she had something like a college trip.'

'So where are they going?' I asked.

Mala shrugged.

'To some hotel, or some military lodge somewhere. Even she doesn't know, I think.'

◆

We travelled to Jamshedpur in the East and spent a week with my parents. They thought Mala a lovely girl and my father proudly talked of my getting married to her a few years after I graduated and was settled with a high-earning job. We said that was, as it stood then, our intention.

We got back to Bombay and the time came for Johnny and me to get back to England and the University. Leaving Mala alone to face her getaway, her virtual elopement, made me feel sick. She was waiting for her passport as Mrs John Snow. She had the fare for a one-way ticket from the sale of my motorcycle.

Once back in Cambridge we exchanged stories of our holiday adventures. Enid had been trekking in Iceland with three other girls. I told her about reconnecting with Mala and about our tryst and the way we had gone about getting her to England.

Enid didn't seem in the least disturbed by my story.

'I thought that's what you intended all along,' she said. She kissed me on the cheek and said it was great that a teenage romance was to progress into the future and that she looked forward to meeting this raven-haired beauty. We decided that from then on our own interaction would be entirely platonic. No more Lawrentian angst and experimentation. No more using that as an excuse, a literary justification for young lusts and yearnings.

The term passed with very many anxious letters from and to Mala. She had been to the British consulate regularly to enquire after her passport. She hadn't given them her women's hostel address or her mother's address so they could inform her about its arrival or dispatch it there. She told them she was travelling and would enquire from time to time.

During the term, I met Dolly, a childhood friend whom I had known from when I was ten or eleven, military brats in Kanpur where my father and hers, an air force officer, were stationed. We had been in touch since our childhood, though she had been to school and college in north India.

Dolly got in touch to say that she was in London for a few years and living in a flat she shared with another girl in Chelsea. She said she was working for the BBC World Service's Hindi section and would love to visit me at Cambridge.

Dolly came and stayed two days. She spent the nights in Enid's room, sharing a bed, and after showing her round the colleges we did the round of the pubs. She said she didn't have a bed to offer me and my friends in London, but there were several second-hand mattresses in their flat and we were welcome to crowd the floors when we came down.

The Christmas holidays were soon upon us and we were required as always to vacate our college rooms. The British boys and girls went home. The rich or well-connected Indians and Pakistanis went to their relatives or to their guardians in the high commissions or abroad on tours to the continent. I went with Johnny to his sister's house in London and several of us, including Johnny and Enid, decided to spend the weekend in Dolly's Chelsea flat.

I was asleep on a mattress on the floor which I was sharing with Enid when Dolly shook me up.

'There's a call from Fershid who got a call from your Mala to say she's at Heathrow airport and on her way here.' We got up in a hurry.

'I think I should go,' Enid said.

'But you must meet her,' I said.

'Not when you're meeting her. Later.' She went back to her family home in South London.

That evening Mala and I walked the pavements of South Kensington looking at the notice boards outside the tobacconist and confectionery shops which advertised rooms to let. We took down the phone numbers and went into the street booths to call them.

Several landlords, landladies and caretakers in these Victorian terraced buildings which were divided up into bedsits on three or four floors, some of them British, some Chinese, some Indian or Pakistani, informed us when we rang the bell that the room had been let. One landlady was honest. She said she wasn't having any Indians as her other tenants would object to sharing bathrooms and toilets with us. She said she was sorry.

I had been told to expect such rejections. Adil and others who had rented rooms said eventually some landlord's need for a tenant would overrule the racism and we'd be in. It did happen. A Pakistani landlord rented us a basement room for three pounds a week and we borrowed that first deposit.

The next day we pawned a gold bracelet which Mala had brought with her in a shop down Fulham Broadway. The money we got for it would set Mala up with a budget for weeks. Dolly said she knew of a vacancy for a salesgirl in the Sari Centre, an Indian garment shop in Soho, and she would call the owner and secure the job for Mala. Mala began work there on the day that term began and we returned to Cambridge.

There was a very distinguished-looking envelope in my pigeonhole. With a sense of foreboding, I took it up to my room to open it. It contained a handwritten letter with a fancy printed address at the top. The letter said:

'*Dear Farrukh Dhondy,*

I am acting on behalf of Mrs B., Mala's mother. Your sly and underhand actions have given her and the family and friends deep distress. Inducing a young woman to jeopardize her life and future in the way that you have done is unforgivable.

As a trustee of the Foundation for the higher Education of Indians which has so generously granted you a scholarship to Cambridge I have to consider the fitness of your character to continue to hold it. You have behaved dishonourably.

We have not been able trace your whereabouts over the winter break and are naturally desperately anxious to get in touch with Mala.

You have to come and see me on 11th January at 4 Cartwright Mansions, Mount Road, Mayfair, London, at 4 p.m. precisely. Till you do, all scholarship payments, including your weekly stipend, are being suspended.

The signature was a flourish with a squiggly line extending from it, the sort of signature which assumes that its fame will overcome its illegibility.

I went to that tryst with my future straight from Cambridge. I said nothing to Mala about it, though we called each other on the phone the day before. I didn't want to perturb her.

I found the flat in Mayfair and loitered ten minutes in the street so that I would ring the bell at precisely 4 p.m. as instructed. A servant let me in. I was shown to a sitting room but thought it prudent, given the nature of the encounter, not to sit down.

The trustee, a tall gentleman in a grey suit, came through the door.

'Yes, Farrukh Dhondy! Sit down.'

He didn't venture a handshake. I sat down. It was Cyclops.

'I believe we have met,' he said.

'Yes, sir, at Mala's mother's house.'

'You have behaved in a most dishonourable way. We don't know if a person of such character should be one of our scholars. There are very many young men and women who are crying out for the privilege we have given you and you abuse it in this way.'

'Sir, there seemed no other way of Mala coming to England and, sir, you know the family and you perhaps know how miserable she was in India. Her father's always away and her mother thinks of nothing but her social standing and puts her daughter in a hostel when she has a house with fifteen bedrooms...'

'How dare you stand in judgement over your superiors – my friends?'

'I am not judging anyone, just reaffirming what you probably know. That Mala has always felt she suffered from a broken family and the bitterness and snobbery...'

'That's quite enough. We are here to judge your actions. You sneaked away and then induced her to sneak away without a thought for the worry it would cause...'

'We had every thought for it. Mala told Fancy, who

accompanied her to the airport, to go straight back and tell her mother where she was and where she was going.'

I was looking straight into Cyclops' face.

'Fancy accompanied her to the airport?'

'I thought she might have told you,' I said.

'You are telling me that Farzana knew about Mala's intentions, your little plot all along?'

'Of course. They are like twins. They share their deepest secrets.'

Cyclops turned visibly pale and for a few seconds, this lion of the Pakistan–India wars averted his eyes from my steady stare. He stood up and paced a few steps, then turned round and looked me in the face.

'Look, Dhondy,' he said. 'Where is Mala now? Is she safe?'

'Of course she is safe.'

'Well, can I see her? Will the two of you come to dinner at... we'll choose a restaurant. Then I can reassure her mother and family. I mean tonight.'

'Certainly, sir. I am sure she'll be delighted.'

He was frowning thoughtfully.

'Farrukh, my boy, we are men of the world and I think we understand each other,' he said.

'Of course, sir,' I said.

'I will of course tell Mrs B that you are both deeply in love and that we must help you to score top marks and get off on a great scientific career and make your relationship with Mala a permanent one.'

'Thank you, sir. There the matter rests.'

'Yes,' he said and extended his hand. 'Would you like a drink? What would you like?'

'Is there any dry sherry?' I asked.

DELIVER THE GOODS

IN MY SECOND Christmas holidays in Britain I determined to earn some money. It was Darryl who directed me to the post office where thousands of students picked up work as temporary staff over the Christmas and New Year period.

Eight of us friends applied together, sending off the forms and finding ourselves assigned to different post offices, jobs and depots in London.

We rented a flat off Edgware Road and piled in there with mattresses, bedding, pots and pans and provisions that would feed the multitude with the least expense. The menu for those weeks was often curry made from sausages or from cans of pilchards which, with rice, potato and cauliflower made into a masala stew, omelettes with potato filling and other inventions, could rival the spread of loaves and fishes in the Bible.

Neither was there any shortage of booze as some of the company assigned to the sorting office or to deliver post would find bottles of whisky, port, gin and brandy sent by corporations to their clients with the labels having come loose. There was no name or address to which to deliver these so they were regarded as common property, confiscated, or 'liberated' and brought to the flat.

Though we got together for drunken evenings and forays out into the snow-laden streets of London, we all had different working hours. I was assigned to a temporary sorting office in the Horticultural Hall in Victoria. It was a huge Victorian building with a porch for the trucks which I and a crew of other students were delegated to load with bags of mail which had been sorted in the hall.

We were porters and had to report for work at 4 a.m. and would spend the next eight to ten hours hauling mailbags to and from the trucks that came and went. Inside the building, other crews of students and regular post office workers who supervised them sorted the mail.

I worked with a crew of seven, all of them students, three of them Africans from the London School of Economics. Our supervisor was a young white post office regular called Andy. He pushed us hard, taunting us with not being able to carry four mailbags at a time – something he demonstrated he could do. Nevertheless, he was generous with our shift and would call 'time' every now and then to give us some rest and sit with us in the canteen next to the hall for a tea or a pastry.

Every morning when we assembled he would tick us off in a register, clap his hands and inevitably greet each one of us with 'Cold, innit?' His gloves covered his palms but let his fingers through so he could hold a clipboard and write on it with the other keeping a tally of our working hours and our breaks. Andy had us as his crew and didn't do any of the lifting himself.

One of the Africans would shuffle rhythmically instead of lifting his feet when hauling the bags. He would sing the same words in a religious tune as he shuffled, repeating the line endlessly every day and through the hours we worked. The burden of his song was 'Oh Jeremiah, oh Jeremiah, oh Jeremiah-ma-ya-ya!' which he rendered in a West African accent as 'Wo jay-ray-maeeyah...'

I never found out his name, but everyone called him Jeremiah and he answered to it.

One day when the seven of us were sitting around in the canteen with Andy for our tea break, Jeremiah addressed me, trying to keep the conversation between us but not quite succeeding as everyone else listened in, breathing steam from the hot tea into the cold air.

'Farroot, you is Indian, yes?'

I said I was.

'In de house where I live in de room above my floor is an Indian gyel. Her name is Kamla and she sing beautiful songs in the night. She is very beautiful and she laugh at me, yes? I pass her on de stairs! She is too beautiful!'

'Yeah, but will she deliver the goods?' Andy asked. 'Right lads, back to the trucks.'

Jeremiah seemed to have stopped singing on that shift and he appeared deep in thought.

The next morning we heard him speaking to himself, muttering under his breath, 'She will deeleevah de goods, she will deeleevah de goods!'

On the last day of our contract Jeremiah was knocked unconscious by a mail truck. It was reversing out of a parking space when its metal back door swung open and hit Jeremiah. He had bad head injuries and was taken straight to hospital. Some of us visited him in hospital the next day and again in the week after. We said we'd keep in touch and exchanged addresses but we never did so; I never found out if Kamla delivered the goods.

YOU WILL CARRY

'GOANCHI, TUJHE MAAL dilwaata hoon, yaar!' I said, as Darryl and I looked down the list of first year undergraduates to spot the names of Indian girls who had come up to Cambridge as freshers. The word 'maal' is laddish slang for goods or merchandise – a derogatory reference to a woman.

We were in our second year, the term had just begun and Mala hadn't yet arrived from India. Darryl was from a distinguished Indian Christian family of Bombay and had been at a fancy private boarding school in the Himalayas. The word 'Goanchi', meaning literally from Goa, was the rough, though not derisory, word we used for all Indian Christians from Western India whether they had any association with Goa or not. Darryl's family, the D'Montes, were certainly not from Goa and were landowners in Bandra, Bombay. His uncle was the editor of the *Times of India* and his cousin was the poet Dom Moraes.

We were looking down the list partly out of a genuine impulse to welcome the new female Indian intake to our crowd and mostly out of mischief. Looking down the list we found three names which were distinctly Indian and marked them. One of them was that of Zareen Jussawala, a girl I had known at college in Poona. It wasn't a common name and couldn't have been anyone but her. The second was called Xena Kabir and the third Yaksha Swamy.

'So X,Y and Z,' Darryl said.

'I know Z. Must be her,' I said.

We noted their colleges and wrote out eccentric invitations to tea in my room and passed through their junior common rooms leaving the invites in their pigeonholes. All three of them accepted. We spent the afternoon buying exotic fruit from the market and making ox-tongue sandwiches for tea.

We had invited a couple of other Indian lads from our year to make up the numbers. The idea was to mildly shock the newcomers with our eccentricity and demonstrate to them that being at a British university didn't mean wearing a tie or assuming a refined English accent or idiom. It was a tiny revolt against the idea, which they would undoubtedly have carried, just as we had, from India, that being at Cambridge was a privilege that set us apart.

The conversation turned to how many undergraduates succumbed to the pressure of competition and went mad. The girls hadn't heard this about the University. I described my visit to the mental hospital outside Cambridge to see David. The girls looked at each other.

'Not a good thing to talk about at tea,' Johnny said, and we switched the subject to the racial attitudes the girls were bound to meet, not just from other undergraduates but from the townspeople, the porters and landladies they would encounter. It was banter calculated to slacken the wind in the sails that had brought them proudly to Cambridge.

The girls caught on. A week later there came counter invitations to tea at Yaksha's rooms. We went.

The girls were there to receive us, wearing pyjamas and dressing gowns.

'We said it was informal, why have you guys come all dressed up?'

On the table with the coffee mugs and the cake, on the single bed and prominently on the seat of one of the chairs we were offered, there were four loose condoms with what must have been cream in their tips. X, Y and Z remained absolutely expressionless as I picked one of them off the chair.

'Shall I get rid of this?' I asked.

'Oh yes, I'll take that, sorry,' Yaksha said.

'We've been getting into the spirit of the University,' Xena added.

Still straight faces all round as Zareen made the coffee and Yaksha deftly removed the 'used' condoms.

'Okay, let's call it quits,' Darryl said and we all burst out laughing. The real conversations began and they told us about their first week and how the Australian undergraduate down their corridor had asked to be shifted from it because, Yaksha heard, she didn't want to share a bathroom and toilet with Indians.

'Did they shift her?'

'No, the senior tutor said it was an absurd request.'

'And did you confront her with it, the Australian?'

'Of course not. What would I say? She's very sweet to our faces – all "Hi! And how was your day?"'

'Maybe it was just a rumour, Chinese whispers!' I said.

'What whispers? Don't be so racist!' Xena said.

◆

When we graduated, Darryl and Zareen spent some time in London. For a while Darryl worked in a southern coastal town as a journalist on the *Kent Messenger*.

When they returned to Bombay, the Big Mango, Darryl started work at the *Times of India* and Zareen worked as an economist and they had Darryl's sumptuous property in Bandra into which they moved when they married.

I was now working in London as a schoolteacher and Mala had a desk job in ticketing for Air India. Her job gave us free flights to India when there were vacant seats on the plane. Our relatives wrote to us fairly regularly asking when they'd see us again. We decided to take a holiday in India. And of course we'd spend time with Darryl and Zareen.

My uncle Khurshed, my 'Mamu', was a civil engineer and owned a building firm. He was convinced that he had picked up the art of palmistry and of drawing up horoscopes and telling people's fortunes. He had managed to convince very many in the family and in his circle of friends of this predictive talent. I had picked up the fact that at the birth of the children of the family he had drawn up our horoscopes which were laid out in diagrams and writing on scrolls of parchment which were then rolled up and tied with coloured ribbon and stowed in the secure drawers of the large mirrored wardrobes in my maternal grandfather's lumbering house in Poona.

I had turned sceptic very early.

This didn't mean that I jettisoned the ethics that religion taught but I was certain that Zoroastrianism's edict of 'good thoughts, good words, good deeds' or Christianity's 'Love thy neighbour' were not the dictates of God but of common sense. And though I could see the value of 'Do unto others as you would have them do unto you', I could also see the irony in the line that the writer of *Jailhouse Rock* puts in the mouth of the character played by Elvis Presley: 'I'm an animal of the jungle and I've got a motto: do unto others as they would do unto you, only do it first!'

I didn't share my uncle's belief in asking God for things through the intervention of holy men, godmen or pirs who millions believed could intercede with the Almighty and even perform miracles.

Some of the beliefs and rituals were harmless and even fun,

but others were bewildering. Whole processions of Muslim Shias passed through the streets at Muharram, the men lashing themselves with blades on chains till their backs bled, the women in full hijab beating their breasts till, I was told, they were sore to the touch.

Our Muslim cook Hookam Ali believed that when the procession of Tazia passed once a year in the night, the tarmac of a particular street by the grave of a saint would tear itself open and fountains would emerge and spread magic water over the procession.

Hindu ritualists would pass, frantically drumming and shouting and leaving behind them limes, chillies and leaves stitched by thread and needle into little dangling bundles or rosettes, believing that whoever stumbled next on to these or touched them with their feet would inherit and be afflicted with any disease from which they or their loved ones suffered. The disease would leave the anointed loved one and enter the body of the hapless stumbler who had kicked the stitched charm.

The cynicism and irreverence a few of my friends and I felt extended to following these processions or approaching the spot and shrines where they had been left as charms, taking the limes home and making jugs of lemonade with water and sugar added to their juice.

Street urchins would follow Hookam Ali from the vegetable market where they had watched him buy a bag of ladies' fingers for the household meal and beg him to spare them the tops and tails of the vegetable when he chopped it so they could take it to their roadside hovel to cook and eat.

There couldn't have been anybody alive there who didn't see this superstition and poverty as my friends and I did, but they made worlds other than the ones we witnessed of the same surroundings.

I loved my Mamu dearly. He was one of the kindest, most balanced humans I knew. I never questioned his faith in astrology or in palmistry though I did make it clear that I didn't believe that bundles of nucleating gases in space or bits of dirt in orbit round them could dictate the lives of human beings. Neither did I believe that the lines on one's palms would have been there if evolution had disposed us to clutch and clench with our feet rather than our hands.

Even so, out of curiosity and idleness and for the company and the ride, I accompanied Khurshed Mamu on visits to a pir, a sage called Kammu Baba whom my uncle and several hundred if not thousands of people, rich, professional, poor and destitute had adopted as a guru, a soothsayer and an intermediary between the troubles, trials and aspirations of their lives and the supernature that governed their fortunes and futures.

When I met Zareen and Darryl on that visit to Bombay we talked about the newspaper stories he was running and the scandals of the time. Then, perhaps a trifle brazenly, I asked them why they hadn't started a family. They said they'd tried, had had themselves medically examined and were assured there was no physical impediment to Zareen's getting pregnant, but it just hadn't happened and it made them sad.

I mentioned this circumstance to Khurshed Mamu and he immediately said that a visit to Kammu Baba would sort it out, adding that he had seen it work in several similar cases. I took this as an ideal opportunity to prove my conviction against effects not having traceable causes. I invited Darryl and Zareen to take up the suggestion and Zareen enthusiastically said she'd try anything, medicinal, irrational, rational, miraculous or unbelievable.

Kammu Baba lived in a shabby bungalow in a shabby compound in Goregaon. On Saturday we set out in Mamu's Fiat car. Kammu's compound was crowded. He was seated on his

indicated that my uncle should distribute the tangerines around the seated audience.

Of a sudden the parrot began to squawk in clear tones:

'*Akela khata hai, akela khata hai, akela khata hai...*' – 'Eating alone, eating alone, eating alone...'

It must have been a studied routine. No one smiled or smirked.

Kammu turned to Khurshed Mamu and calling him by his surname said to him in Gujarati, 'Antia, myna limbu maagech!' – 'Antia, the myna bird is asking for a lime.'

That he had categorized the bird and the fruit wrongly didn't seem to concern him or my uncle or anyone else. After all he wasn't a botanist or ornithologist, he was a saint. My uncle peeled a tangerine and fed the bird.

Kammu got nimbly off the charpoy, gathering his lungi with his left hand thrust between his legs and held out his hand to Zareen. He nodded to Darryl to indicate that he knew why they were there.

He led Zareen into the garden and they walked together round the little orchard. We watched from afar. He held both her hands and, she told us later, breathed or muttered an invocation into them. He then announced to her, 'You will carry!'

The three of us walked around the compound while Mamu confided his business worries to the Baba. When they were done we went to say goodbye. He held our hands in turn and as we left, he shouted after us, 'Carry on!'

Three months later, back in London, I received the news by letter that Zareen was indeed 'carrying'.

CALIGULA

IN MY SECOND year, the Pembroke Players asked me to direct the annual play. I was a member of this college drama group and directed end-of-term plays and skits, drawing on my experience of amateur dramatics from college back in India.

I wasn't an aspirant actor or director. If anything, I wanted to write for the theatre one day, some day! I was acutely conscious that I could parody any contemporary playwright from the absurdities of Harold Pinter or the philosophical-sounding nothings of Samuel Beckett to the puzzles of Pirandello, but was also aware that whatever I wrote in this vein would be transparently derivative. I hadn't found my material but told myself that my material hadn't found me.

The truth of course was that I had nothing dramatic to say to a British audience. The closest I got to inventing a play that would work here was to take a theme from British Indian colonialism and present the story through the perspective of an Indian. The Raj through Indian eyes might startle. The one story I hit upon then and began to write in my second year at the University was the impeachment by the Westminster parliament of Warren Hastings, Governor General of Bengal and the East India Company's territories in India, for corruption, extortion and related crimes. I would, I thought, introduce Indian witnesses who weren't in reality called and have a chorus of Indian street musicians and experiment with absurdist or surrealist form.

I read about the trial in the University library, took diligent notes but it never happened. The play never materialized and I put that down at the time to being busy with my study of Physics and solving the maths papers I had to submit to tutors. Later it became clear again that I had no clarity about what I wanted to say about Warren Hastings or about British colonialism or anything else. To say it was unjust and exploitative would be a cliché and I would lose momentum as I wrote. So no play.

Years later I realized that the study of English is all about criticism and not about creativity. In a very important sense, the critical enterprise inhibits creative writing which originates in a non-rational impulse or at least through a channel of the subconscious. Criticism is consciously tracing the mechanism and placing the worth of a poem or novel or play. The logical, critical mind is at some level involved in the act of creative writing but its impulse and inspiration, even its discipline originate elsewhere.

I had thought of writing the play and trying to have it produced by the Players but then, for these reasons, given up the thought. Then, out of the blue, Donald, a third year classics scholar and the year's artistic director of the Players, approached me in Hall and said they would like to speak to me over a drink at one of the college pubs later.

Four members of the Players' committee – Donald, Mike, Celia and Donald's girlfriend Naomi – bought me several drinks and asked if I'd consider directing the year-end play which was to be Albert Camus' *Caligula*. I knew the play and was flattered to be asked as they laid it on quite thick by saying they had considered ten potential directors and thought about putting the role out to tender and subsequent interviews but there was a strong feeling that I was to be approached without the process as they were convinced I was the best person... Of course it was flattering but I responded by asking them how many people they had really approached and why they had turned it down.

Donald looked genuinely insulted. He frowned.

'Come on, Dhondy, stop fishing. You are genuinely the only choice and you say you've read the play and like it.'

'We've brought a copy in the unlikely event that you hadn't,' Naomi said. 'I mean if you weren't familiar with it.'

I took the copy of the Penguin paperback she had.

'I'll go through it tonight, but great! I am surprised but thankful for the compliment. Of course I'll do it. When do we start?'

'Auditions in a few days, we'll put out ads, but you know our regular talent pool and you can give me a list and we'll get hold of them. And you can say what times suit you. Auditions in the Old Library which Meredith says we can use for rehearsals any time. Performance? A week in June after the Tripos. We'll line up the lighting, set design, costume and make-up and publicity crew as usual. Plenty of volunteers.'

'Sounds good!'

We drank to Caligula and his horse and to existentialism – we were nothing if not pretentious.

I auditioned twenty people to play Caligula. A young actor called Nick, in his first year, studying Moral Sciences, which is Cambridge's name for theology, was startling in the confidence, cunning and Machiavellian clowning which the part, as I interpreted it, demanded. The Penguin English translation from the French was, the lecturer in the Modern Languages department told me one day at dinner, more dramatic than the original. That was good.

The plan was to rehearse for several weeks in the Easter term and then break for two weeks or ten days before exams and then resume rehearsals for ten days after, when the undergraduate world, freed of its anxieties, would be partying, punting and picnicking.

By the time we got to the study break, rehearsals had come to near perfection, the sets were being constructed, and the production and stage crews were all on board and knew what they were doing. With the exams over, I called the cast and crew. The posters, with the helmeted head of Caligula, were all over Cambridge.

Rehearsals were running smoothly. The play and my, or our, vision of it improved every day. And then I got the flu. I was living at the time in the attic of an empty house, rent-free, as the couple who owned it, a young don and scientist and his Indian wife, were away for a few months in the USA. They had let me stay provided I made my nest in the attic which I had to clear of its clutter and paint as part of the deal.

While I was in bed, nursing the flu, Naomi came with the final designs for the set and the details of the hundred props we were accumulating or the art contingent was fabricating in modernistic interpretations of Roman style.

Naomi was at Newham College doing her final year in Archaeology and Anthropology. Since our colleges were gender segregated, the Pembroke Players solicited members and actresses from the women's colleges and the tradition had been long established that each year the veteran women members would bring along others. There was no shortage of volunteers as the Players had a good reputation.

Naomi was, in accent and demeanour, of the rural, landowning upper class of England. She was a devout Catholic with patrician features, unruly blonde hair which would fall over her face, with its straight parody of a nose, bright eyes which betrayed every phase her brain underwent and a smile that turned the end of her broad lips downward. She was and had been Donald's girlfriend from their first term. I knew they had met in the Pembroke Players and their relationship had lasted through their three years.

I took her up to the attic, my habitation where I had begun the painting of the walls with a stepladder and several cans of light blue paint. She asked after my health as we climbed the stairs and I admitted that I had actually fully recovered, that I was confident that the play was ready and needed my time to finish painting the wretched room. She was amused.

'Shamming!' she said.

'I'm afraid so, but all for a good cause. The battle goes on though Achilles sulks in his tent. I'll be back tomorrow, promise.'

'Don't you have to finish painting your attic?'

'Suppose I'll have to admit failure on that score,' I said.

She surveyed the room.

'You've done most of it. Come on, let's finish it,' she said.

It took me a brief moment to appreciate that she was offering to help me paint. I was about to say 'no need for that' when she approached and put the artwork she had brought for me down on my bed and pried open a can of paint and took up a brush.

'You're really going to do it?'

'Yes, watch me, but I can't afford to get this dress in a mess with paint.' So saying she pulled her tight-hipped dress over her head, wriggling her hips to facilitate its movement upwards, and threw it on the bed. She was now in her knickers, bra and socks and shoes. She kicked her shoes off and matter-of-factly mixed the paint with the brush and having chosen her section of the wall began painting it.

I was stunned by the adolescent uninhibitedness of it, but then that's what the confidence of her class had given her. I would have betted that her father would have hunted with hounds or even been the master of a hunt and that he would have been shooting partridge in the late autumn, but I would have lost the bet.

'Tell me about yourself,' she said as we both painted away.

I struggled to keep my eyes on the painting and off her body with its perfectly nestling breasts, flat abdomen and hips broad enough to be childbearing and bony enough to give a hint of boyishness. It was her own individual perfection and she seemed confident in the knowledge that she possessed it.

My reading of English books and magazines in India had given me a rough if erroneous view of what British people would be like. P.G. Wodehouse's people, despite the caricatures, seemed to me, on acquaintance with Britain, a shallow but accurate characterization of the Britain that I was as yet unacquainted with.

Apart from John Snow and his upper-class and expat eccentric family – his father was a doctor who lived in the Middle East, his aunt was a nun in Bombay, his sister had married a Pakistani doctor and lived in Manchester and his other sister was the closest an upper-class girl could be to an American beatnik – I knew or was intimate with very few county types.

Naomi was distinctly one and when I had told her a little about myself and my origins, which is what she seemed fascinated by, putting down her paintbrush and facing me as I continued to paint and speak, I asked her to tell me about herself.

She described her large shambolic house and her unhappiness at boarding school where she was supervised by nuns who characterized Elvis Presley and Bobby Darin as the devil's messengers. Her father was deeply Catholic and he was opposed to hunts though he did own horses and a pack of dogs.

We finished the painting and briefly discussed the sets and sketches she had brought in a folder. She hadn't put on her dress and was still in her underwear; I thought she was quietly proud of the strong attraction to her half-naked body which I was desperately but unsuccessfully trying to cover up. She sat on my bed making no move to leave and get on with her evening.

'Tell me what you thought about London when you first got there,' she said.

I didn't think I should sit on the bed next to her and I self-consciously wandered to the attic window set in the sloping roof wall, pretending to draw the curtains to prevent the full glare of the sun which now shone directly through it.

'Leave the curtain; I want to watch the sun setting. And if it rains again we can watch the rainbow and hold hands and make two wishes – or maybe it'll be just one. So stay there and talk to me, apostle of the East! About first impressions. London!' She propped up her legs on the bed and closed her eyes lightly as she might have done as a little girl when her nanny was telling her a bedtime story.

'I suppose in some recess of my mind I was expecting Dickensian buildings, but on the way in from the airport there were only rows and rows of Edwardian terraced houses and I was quite ... um ... disconcerted. Till we hit the centre of town and the Victorian architecture began. E.M. Forster calls the outer spread of the city "the rust of London".'

'So who was the first person you met in England?'

'If you mean "met" met – talked to properly – I'll tell you. I spent my first few nights in London in a rooming house in Cathcart Road in South Ken. The landlady showed me to my room and then in the evening knocked at my door to say dinner was served in the basement. I went down to the dining room where there were two tables and eight chairs and a hatch leading to the kitchen through which her husband was dishing out plates of meat and two veg to the residents.

'I got my plates and sat down but my attention was fixed to

the corner of the room where a TV set was booming out music. I had never seen TV before. It was tuned to what I later discovered was Top of the Pops and Diana Ross and The Supremes and these four beautiful black girls were belting out "Baby, baby, where did our love go?"

'A young man, about the same age as me, came and sat opposite me. He had a Mod haircut and was wearing a grey Mod-styled jacket.

"You a soul freak?" he asked.

'I had no idea what the words meant.'

Naomi laughed. 'How would you?'

'That was the first person I met. He asked me if I'd ever been to a pub and I said I'd only arrived that afternoon. Then he asked me if I drank alcohol and said he'd take me to a pub after dinner. I said I'd like that and went round the corner. He said he was from Liverpool and stayed in the same rooming house once a month when he came down to London on some sales business.'

'Was he trying to pick you up?' Naomi asked.

'No, no, no. Why would he?'

'I would have if I was him,' she said.

I didn't know what to say to that. I walked away from the window. The sun was now low and shone straight in her face.

'Come with me,' I said.

I led her, in her undress, down the stairs, through the drawing room on the ground floor, through the kitchen and into the basement where there was the family's wine cellar – rows of white and red wines.

'You choose, I don't know much about wines.'

She chose a wine which said Chateau something or other but she called it claret.

We went back up to the attic and drank the wine and talked. We talked into the night about nothing and everything. She was charpoy on a side veranda of the house. A door led into a darkened room. Outside the door, above the charpoy hung a silver bird cage with a large parrot, asleep, or resting with his eyes shut on a swinging wooden perch. There were perhaps sixty people sitting in rows on the floor of the veranda. Others, who had come simply to have a glimpse of the Master, sat or crouched in groups around the grounds, some in the little grove of fruit trees at the side of the bungalow.

Kammu wore a checked lungi and a loose kurta with a hanky tied in a cap around his head with the knot to one side. On seeing my uncle, Kammu summoned him to the front of the crowd to sit on the charpoy next to him. The three of us followed and the newcomers were introduced.

'Ah, Darryl Dee Mownty?' Kammu remarked, as though he had uniquely recognized a Catholic name. He stuck the thumb of his right fist out and put it to his lips, mimicking a swig from a bottle and with a twinkle in his eye asked, '*Kitna peg?*'

Had he guessed that Zareen and Darryl had come to talk about a desired pregnancy? Was he asking about Darryl's consumption of alcohol to imply erectile dysfunction or low sperm count owing to high alcohol levels? These questions flashed through my mind, but I concluded that Kammu was just being mischievous and stereotyping Darryl as a Catholic Goan who liked his quota of hooch per day.

Another disciple walked in with an offering, a small basket with a dozen tangerines in it. Kammu motioned him to wade through the audience and come to the front. He indicated that my uncle should accept the gift basket and he held his hand out for a tangerine. He appeared to bless it, peeled it, threw the peel aside on the bed and, separating the segments, handed them first to Zareen and then in turn to us and the others in the front row. He in a confessional mood and said she had been with Donald all through her three years.

'That's great,' I said.

'In some ways, but I came up expecting to have lots of ups and downs of relationships, you know? But being with one bloke it's like a plateau, a bit flat.'

'Spares the heartache,' I said.

'But it's like being married too early and allowing the sleep to overtake you too early.'

'The sleep?'

'It's what we – my mates – call it; the boredom, but not exactly, just the unexciting continuity.'

'So what would be exciting?'

'To not go back to college tonight. To spend the night with you!'

I could have seen it coming and the proposition made my pulse run faster.

'So get another bottle of – what do you call it, claret? I usually drink beer and of course sherry.'

'No, don't get any wine. I want to stay sober for this,' she said.

Her face said she had made up her mind to go through with this experiment, a last fling to compensate for all the relationships she should or could have had with different men in the three years she had spent faithfully with Donald.

She stood up and undid her bra and nimbly took her knickers off, raising her knees. She pulled the duvet back and got into bed conscious that I was spellbound, watching her.

'So?' she asked sitting up in bed, her firm small boyish breasts protruding above the edge of the duvet.

I took my clothes off and got into bed beside her. I got out again to turn the light out but she touched me on my back.

'Leave the light on, at least for a bit.'

Did I have any pangs of disloyalty? No, not then. She made love impatiently, wanting no persuasion, no foreplay. She kissed me with her eyes shut and held my erection to ascertain, perhaps, if I reciprocated her impatience or perhaps to stimulate me into satisfying her impatience. Her hips moved up and down spontaneously as she lay on her back.

I hadn't pulled the curtains and the dull morning light woke us up. We had made love through the night with Naomi waking me up from my bouts of sleep, finally getting on top of me and inducing, even forcing, my erection by rubbing my half-inclined prick against her wetness.

As the light of the morning brightened, she asked where the shower was. We showered together, got dressed and I offered her breakfast. We went downstairs and had coffee. She said nothing about the night or its adventure but she smiled and kissed my forehead when we sat down on the high kitchen stools.

Donald was sitting in his VW Beetle on the opposite side of the road when we walked out of the house. There were other parked cars but no traffic on the road at that early hour. I didn't notice his car, Naomi did.

'Oh shit!'

'What?'

'Donald!'

He didn't turn the window of the driver's seat down. He sat there looking straight ahead. I could see she was wondering whether she should pretend she hadn't seen him and walk away or whether she should go up to the car.

'Don't come with me,' she said. She had decided. I watched as she went and tapped at his car window. He had his head bent over the steering wheel now, his hands clutched above his head.

She went to the other side of the car and got in. He didn't glance towards me as he started the car and drove her away.

I'd come out to walk her home and perhaps have breakfast in Hall at my college, but I turned back and went into the house. Only then did I see a scrap of paper to the side of the doormat. We hadn't noticed it on leaving. I picked it up.

Though the paper was a scrap torn out of a motor car log book, it was a neat and deliberate note. At the top was the time: 01.39 a.m. It said, 'Expect the anthropological research is going intimately and well.

The anticipated betrayal is evidence of good character judgement. The unexpected betrayal is a lesson in life. (Not translated from the Greek of anyone.)

Please don't either of you come back to the rehearsals, if only to avoid a public embarrassment and to spare the feelings of one who offered you nothing but respect.'

It wasn't signed. It was to the both of us, to his Naomi and to me.

I thought about his demand or was it just a request? I stayed in that day not wanting to go near college where the crew would be rehearsing probably under the guidance of Donald and, perhaps without Naomi, putting the finishing touches to her designs. Donald would have to make up excuses for both our sudden absences.

I lay in bed reading. The night had been exhausting if exhilarating and now the guilt began to creep in. Yes, the whole pent-up current of frustration emerged in that night. The expectation she may have had when she first came to the University, of a life of romance and illicit encounters had turned into a steady single liaison which was now possibly like a stale marriage. And so this last fling!

But would it be the last? Now that Donald would cut her loose, end their relationship, a compelling tragedy for him, would she go out of the shelter of the University into the larger world with new expectations? Had the experiment with me kindled new flames or reminded the dried gullet of the satisfaction of slaking a thirst?

And me? I put it out of my mind. It had been nothing beyond finding out about an intriguing personality. Yes, I could have, under different circumstances or stars, fallen in love with Naomi, but apart from an entrance into a different stratum of British life, what would she offer me? Yes, if life was only about love, one could get on with another, whoever the one and the other, but it isn't.

I stayed away from the rehearsals and only went into college in the mornings. I encountered two or three Pembroke Players who were surprised to see me. They said they'd thought I'd left town and asked after my sister and her operation. I don't know what Donald had told them. Yes, I did have a sister and yes she did have a heart operation in London in my first year at the University, but the only person to whom I had recounted an incident at the hospital was, that night of reminiscence, Naomi.

I dodged the questions, saying yes, my sister was by no means out of danger post-operation and I would have to go back to London. I stayed away from college and only went in to town to replenish my stock of food to cook. The poster for *Caligula* had black stickers reminding people of the dates of the production and telling them that four of the shows out of six had already been sold out. So at least that was looking good. Donald must have taken over the design and the direction.

On the afternoon of the day on which the first performance was scheduled, the doorbell rang. I went down the stairs to answer it.

Donald and Naomi were at the door.

'May we come in?' Donald asked.

I nodded, intrigued. We stood in the hallway.

'I've stayed away,' I protested.

'This is urgent, Farrukh, we've come with a request, please!' Naomi said.

'You have to help us out – yourself, your brilliantly directed production,' Donald added.

I didn't understand.

'Come in, sit down, explain,' I said.

I wanted to ask how they were together, what had transpired after she got into his Beetle and drove away that morning. I think Naomi understood, reading the question in my mind because she shook her head ever so slightly to indicate that this was not the time.

Donald may have seen the same question because he ventured to side-step it.

'We've talked it over and decided she used you. Sorry, but let's forget about it and get on,' he said.

'Nick's had a nervous breakdown and been carted off to a...' she couldn't say it.

'To a mental hospital in Wales, for God's sake. He went for his mother's wedding to some fellow that Nick disapproves of. He told me before he went two nights ago and swore he'd be back this morning, fresh and ready. His older sister phoned. He attacked his mum's bridegroom at the wedding and had a breakdown.'

'So *Caligula* is fucked,' I said. 'After all that!'

'It's not if you can play the character, play Caligula,' Naomi said.

It was the last thing I had expected to hear.

'You are the only person who knows the lines word-perfect and who knows what the director wants out of the character and action,' Donald said.

'But I'm not an actor. I've never acted, except as a girl in Oscar Wilde's *The Canterville Ghost* in school in India, when I was twelve.'

'Naomi and I and the rest of the cast whom we've just met with have no doubt you can do it. They said you used to step into roles while rehearsing. In fact two or three of them suggested it as soon as we gave them the bad news.'

I stood up and felt compelled to pace the room.

'You throw me out, then you come to ask me to play the fucking main role,' I said.

'I know how you feel. You probably know how I feel,' Donald said, 'but put that away and think of the Pembroke Players. This year's members will be gone and you and Mike and Celia will be in virtual charge of the company.'

'Please?' Naomi said. They really had come to plead, expecting my negativity, and I felt the best course would be to surprise them and give them none.

'Of course I'll play Caligula – and his horse. But do I have to wear the wretched toga.'

'Are you calling my designed costume a toga?' Naomi asked.

'Nick looked terribly Anglo-Saxon in it. You'll look more Mediterranean,' Donald said.

'But my stubble? Do I have to shave?' I asked.

'Ask your designer,' Donald said.

'I think that would be too much to ask,' Naomi said. 'Keep the stubble; it's charming.'

I don't think Donald wanted her to say that last word.

The cast were very welcoming. The senior common room had been turned into the costume, make-up and even flats and props room. The Hall had been converted into a theatre and the stage for high table had been raised to theatrical levels.

As we were preparing, Donald addressed the audience, telling them about the change of cast. Half-jokingly, he offered them a refund if as a consequence they wanted to leave. The hall was full and no one left. They may have been curious.

I had contrived a small change at the last minute. I would enter the stage with a book in my hand implying to the audience that I needed to read the script as I hadn't memorized it.

It had precisely that effect. I couldn't see the audience's faces as the footlights were on and blinded me, but Naomi told me later that for half a minute as she watched the audience anxiously while I pretended to read out my lines, it's what they seemed to assume. Then, at the point where I had a longish monologue, I flamboyantly flung the book away and delivered my lines, word-perfectly. The gesture would be, I thought, part of the eccentricity or madness that Camus had written in to Caligula. The last thing I expected as I launched into my monologue was the audience breaking into loud applause, to encourage the substitute Caligula and indicate that they weren't disappointed. Every time there was a dramatic turn in my performance they repeated the applause. It was quite disconcerting, if ego boosting.

Donald hugged me after the performance and Naomi followed. The cast were overjoyed. Some of them said I was much better at being the Big C than Nick.

All six performances went off well.

Nick returned to Cambridge looking wan and weary, with hollow cheeks. He watched the final performance and came to congratulate me and the cast afterwards.

Was I going to take up acting after Uni, he asked.

No, I said, but I knew he wanted to and I said he absolutely should.

He did. Years later I saw him frequently on TV, but never in a starring role.

TASSELS AND TUSSLES

ON THE WEEKENDS when I didn't hitch rides to London, standing on the road at Trumpington Street and sticking a thumb out at passing cars, Mala would take the train to Cambridge.

When I lived in the attic of the family that was away, we had the run of the house, but that was only for a few weeks till they returned from the States. Then I found digs in a house near the station. The landlady made it very clear from the moment I stepped into her house, 'There's to be no hanky-panky here in my house. You may have guests but they have to leave by dinner time which means seven-thirty, young man.' As she showed me to the room she outlined the rules by which her 'guests', as she called me and an older man, who lived in the bedroom below mine, were expected to live.

It was discomfort at first sight. She was a large overbearing woman with thick arms and thick legs under slinky skirts too short for her frame or her age. Her front room into which I glanced had maroon sofas with maroon tassels hanging off them. The curtains were dark blue and again had tassels hanging from them as did the sash which pulled them together. The colours looked oppressive in the small room, forbidden to the guests.

We were restricted to the neat hall with a hat stand hung

with a single coat and a single ladies' hat, to the staircases and the landings and our own rented rooms. Porcelain dogs hung on the side of the carpeted staircase. My room was on the second floor of her narrow three-bedroom house.

I was out most of the day and in the evenings and came back to the room only to sleep. It didn't feel as though I could possess it in any way. It had prints and photographs of racehorses framed on the walls and a blue bedcover with tassels at the end. I had my own bathroom which was the only attractive asset to the rent. I had looked around for other rooms but this was the only vacant one on offer at mid-term.

It had a kettle and I could wash my mugs in the bathroom basin. There was nowhere to cook or heat food so for those weeks I skipped lunch and ate dinner in Hall.

Mala came one evening on a Friday. I picked her up at the station and we took a walk into town to meet Darryl, Zareen, Mathai, Dickie, Ian, Yaksha and John at a pub. We ate an Indian meal at a restaurant and the plan was that Mala would go back to Zareen's hostel where she could sleep in the room without problems as no supervisor lived on the premises.

However, after dinner Mala, with her rucksack of clothing, clung to my arm and asked why we couldn't stay together.

'I don't think Zareen would want me in her rooms too,' I said.

'I mean go back to your room,' she said.

'You don't know what Lady Tassel is like. It's absolutely forbidden to have a guest after seven-thirty, her dinner time, as she put it.'

'So by eleven she'll be asleep and we can sneak up,' Mala said.

'And when do we sneak down?' I asked.

'We can all come in a gang for coffee at your place in the morning, say nine o'clock and then we come down in a crowd with you too,' Yaksha suggested.

The rest agreed.

'Go on, dare you, just don't make noise while making love,' Dickie said.

'It'll look odd all of you turning up,' I said.

'We'll manage that, as long as there are the two girls,' Ian said.

Mala started literally jumping up and down.

The ruse worked till the last moment. I came down the stairs and let them in when they rang the bell in the morning. Lady Tassel came to the hall door in an apron and went back to her cooking or breakfast when I said it was okay, they were guests I was expecting for coffee as we were all off to watch an Oxbridge cricket match.

Three men and two girls followed me upstairs. We did boil the kettle and had coffee and then traipsed downstairs. Lady Tassel was waiting in the hall as we came down the stairs, hastily heading for the front door.

'Not so fast. I counted as these people went up,' she said. She pointed at Mala who was on the staircase as all of us had stopped in our tracks.

'That girl stayed here overnight,' Lady Tassel said.

'Gosh, darling,' Ian said. 'You should enter the championship of Kim's game, you know, where you have to remember objects on a tray.'

She had her fists on her hips. 'Get out of my house,' she said. 'And I shall be speaking to your college. You have an hour to get your things out.'

'I'll be down in ten minutes, hang about,' I said to the company.

Mala followed me upstairs. I had a suitcase and a bag for my books and records and Dickie and Ian came up and we hauled my worldly possessions down and out of the house, watched by Lady Tassel from the bottom of the stairs.

'Thank you for your kindness, Lady Tassel,' were my last words to her.

'Get your whore out of my house,' she said.

We deposited my bags at the Porters' Lodge in college. The head porter with whom I was on friendly terms asked me whether I was on my way out.

'No,' I said, 'I've been thrown out of my digs for having my girlfriend there overnight.'

'Now that is naughty but nice, Mr Farrukh,' he said in his Irish accent.

That evening I found a note in my pigeonhole summoning me to see Meredith Dewey, my tutor. I went up to his rooms.

'So what's all this about? You've been rusticated! Have a drink, dear fellow. Give us the goss. Who was the girl? University? Town?'

'No, no, my fiancée from India.'

'You broke the rules,' he said, giving me a glass of dry sherry and indicating that I should sit down.

'So where are you going to live?'

'I don't yet know. I'll find a bunk for the night and go to the University lodgings place in the morning.'

'Your landlady spoke to Hazel and demanded to speak to me, but I don't speak to landladies,' he said, taking his pipe out of his mouth. 'I find charging money for the use of space as repulsive as charging money for breathing.'

'It's the laws of property, which, as you have heard, is theft.'

'You Marxists are infuriating and only half right,' he said. 'But I have a suggestion. You should move into the college guest rooms till you find some digs.'

It was very kind of him. The guest rooms were meant for visiting dignitaries and he was offering one to a delinquent undergraduate.

'And I presume your young lady is accommodated.'

'Gone back to London,' I said.

'For the best,' he said. 'Get Johnson to assign the small room to you.'

I lived in the college guest room for five days. The word that I had been caught with a woman in my rooms and expelled from my lodgings had spread throughout the college. Glances, remarks and several querying conversations told me that I had gained an enviable notoriety. The first years, I fancied, regarded me with awe and respect. I heard a few completely nonsensical rumours about having held an all-night oriental orgy with group participation in my rooms. At any rate I had broken the cardinal rule of celibacy that was a leftover of the monkish ancestry of Cambridge and I had avoided the fall. It was as though Adam had eaten the apple and was being treated as a horticultural expert on apple varieties.

It was Mathai who found the shabby little house for rent at the end of Trafalgar Street from a very old, very bent, very deaf and very absent and non-interfering lady. He came to the college and said my need had prompted him to look, and in his energetic and sometimes unnecessarily secretive way he had gone about looking for places which would reduce the money he paid for his Churchill college rooms and which we could share. He found it through the University's lodging facility.

The house – two bedrooms and the bath upstairs and a front room and a back room, which was a kitchen, and the dining room downstairs – was cheap, dirty and disgustingly maintained by the undergraduates who had just moved out. All three were famous in University circles, two men and a woman who were the stars of the main productions that year at ADC. They were all destined for great careers as thespians.

They had left the house in a dreadful state. The mattresses

in each room were laid on the floor with stuffing coming out of holes which could easily have bred mice. There was one wardrobe upstairs which fell apart when we opened the door. The bath and toilet looked, with their lime scale and thick yellow coating, as though they were part of a public toilet in an Indian bazaar. The kitchen was thick with grease and grime, and no birds sang.

Mala came from London. We threw their mattresses, carrying them, loaded precariously, wobbling and being wheeled, struggling on our bicycles to the dump. We scrubbed and cleaned and bought second-hand furniture and set ourselves up as householders, with me in the front room on the first floor and Mathai in the room overlooking the small yard.

Now Mala could visit whenever she could and our front room on the ground floor became a guest room for all our friends who wanted to bring a mate to spend a night. Needless to say, the facility in the restrictive Cambridge of the day was much used and much appreciated.

BECKET

IF BRITAIN IS about anything it's about class, but it is sophisticatedly so, constantly and ambivalently attempting to demonstrate that it doesn't matter, that it's a cultural reality but a socio-political irrelevance. This attempt invokes the semi-mythological contention that the country, since the Second World War at least, is a meritocracy. Britain boasts the fact that the humblest born have risen to prominence and wealth in every field from Lord Denning who was a Lord Chief Justice to Alan Sugar who is an entrepreneur millionaire to David Davis who narrowly missed leading the Tory Party. Then of course there was the grocer's daughter who became prime minister and the lower-middle-class grammar school boy who preceded her.

The fact is that class fuels snobbery in both directions. Pop singers and rock stars with distinctly middle-class and even suburban origins pose as working-class rebels and alter their accents accordingly. The nouveau riche take up county sports and buy aristocratic houses. Every toff has a favourite soccer team and millions of plebs fill the rugby stadiums though very rarely the Albert Hall for the Promenade Concerts.

In my time in Cambridge there was a smattering of boys and girls who were from the genuine early generations of meritocracy, by which I mean they had promoted themselves by academic achievement from an early age to entry into universities which a few generations before them wouldn't have admitted their kind or class. Yes, there was a clear antagonism from some of them to the traditions of the University and certainly towards the openly demonstrative upper-middle-class public school generation. The tension seldom broke out in open antagonism but it was distinctly there and it invited the likes of me to choose. It wasn't a difficult choice; being a colonial of a particular class, I never felt at home with the pranks, predilections and prejudices of the distinctly accented fraternities of the rugger-buggers or the rowing crews. I had to side with, and sidle up to, the donkey-jacketed brigade and did.

Just having got to Cambridge or Oxford left these working-class lads and lasses in strange dilemmas. The study and pursuit of literature, drama, the arts, modern languages and philosophy, which was quaintly labelled 'Moral Sciences', couldn't be characterized as any traitorous proclivity. The acquisition or love of any of these didn't paint you as a snob. But it did, by dint of the historical development of Britain, isolate you in some ways from the culture, preoccupations and even prejudices of your working-class background and family.

The experience of the first socially engineered generation of meritocrats in Britain, the miners' sons who went to university, say, even gave rise to the genre of literature labelled kitchen sink. The plays and the novels of this school featured the educated lad who felt alienated from his barely literate working class father. The extreme example, decades after the kitchen sink's heyday, was the film and subsequent West End play *Billy Eliot* in which a young man wants to be a ballet dancer and knows he is gay and has to battle the absolute incomprehension of his miner father and elder brother who are suffering in a fight-to-the-finish industrial battle over the mines.

Several of my working-class friends at the University, including Dave, blithely assumed that kitchen sink literature was about them and there was no escape from the predicament that the cultures of class had imposed on them. They thought of the genre of novels and plays as the natural dramatic expression of their Britain. Their Britain, and by God, they wanted to fight the upper classes for the ownership of it.

An English graduate's father may never have thought Hamlet was a mispronunciation, but he may quite plausibly have thought that *The Waste Land* was a council report on the plot behind the derelict mine.

Some were militantly bitter. Ian, whom I met as he lived in the Bull Hostel of St Catherine's in the room next to Darryl, introduced me to his friend Greg Benton who was studying Chinese and was full of Maoist rhetoric. He had a scar on his cheek and even at the age of twenty a receding hairline. And he was bitter.

Weeks after I met him with Ian and argued over a beer whether the revolution sparked by Maoists would overtake India, a newsworthy political protest hit Cambridge. Overnight someone had painted in huge ten foot writing on the side of King's College chapel, the most famous building in the university, 'FREE MANDELA!' It was a slogan with which the body of the University, undergraduates and seniors would have agreed, but painting the slogan on the chapel was an act of vandalism. Greg was indicted as one of the perpetrators or painters. He was hauled before some University or college tribunal and rusticated for a year. The adjudicators recognized that these were working-class lads with a passion for the rights and wrongs of world politics. Greg would go down for a year but would return and resume his Chinese studies.

He became, when I last heard, a professor of Chinese at Leeds University, though he may have preferred to have led the workers of Britain to enforce a dictatorship of the proletariat. That was precisely the dilemma of the angry meritocrats of that time – they were isolates and though their number was destined to grow, they had no army behind them and couldn't lead their parents' generation from whom they were culturally estranged into some British class war.

◆

In a drama production in Cambridge, the idea of divisions between the middle and working class would be absurd. The Pembroke Players, after the *Caligula* episode, invited me to direct T.S. Eliot's *Murder in the Cathedral* about the martyrdom of Thomas Becket for a tour of West Germany, East Berlin and two venues in Poland.

The administrative experts of the Players, Michael and Celia, had fixed the coach transport, the route, the venues, the finances and the arrangements to obtain visas and all they needed was a play. The venues at which the projected tour would perform had come after long back-and-forth discussion, I was told, and these venues had opted for T.S. Eliot and *Murder in the Cathedral*. Would I do it?

I said yes, not least because Mala said she'd like to come along as a stagehand and see Germany and Poland.

Auditions began and a mixture of talent from all over the University applied. It would be a free travel holiday and a prestigious tour.

I cast the play fully aware that Ian, who was to star as Becket, had an enduring contempt for upper-class 'twits' as he called them, but he had the forbearance to treat his disdain with restraint and tact. One of the murderous knights I cast was none other than Bill Thomas, he of the varsity boat race scam.

The female chorus had three very discernibly middle-class actors and two who were distinctly and defiantly not. The cast and crew numbered thirty-two people.

We crossed the channel by ferry. The cast and crew had become a friendly dynamic unit over the period of rehearsal and we weren't travelling as a tour group but as a gang or gaggle of friends. We'd share large bottles of Coke and cider and even mixes of gin and tonic or rum and ginger which one or the other of the party would concoct. Bill Thomas's cry from the last seat in the coach which he had pointedly reserved for himself, as the bottles were passed around from person to person and mouth to mouth was 'No slobbering!' He took it upon himself from time to time to stand in the aisle of the moving coach and demonstrate, much as air hostesses do on safety drills, how to hold the bottle a good six inches above your head while pouring the drink into your mouth.

We performed in two cities to thronged audiences of university students before we hit Berlin. We spent our nights in youth hostels and cheap accommodation and all went smoothly. We explored the nightlife of the cities as we went in smaller intimate groups of the special friends we'd made.

The performance in West Berlin, again packed out and vastly appreciative, was in the blue cathedral on the main drag, the Kurfurstendamm.

On the third day in Berlin, our coach went through Checkpoint Charlie into East Berlin. Our coach was escorted into the walled city by students from its university. The contrast with West Berlin's neon and rebuild was startling, but here, with its monumental buildings and boulevards, was magnificent Berlin. We performed to a packed house of a disciplined East German University crowd, who applauded at the end only, seemingly after the signal from, I suppose, some student commissar.

We were given a meal in a basement hall with trestle tables at which perhaps a thousand young people were seated for a meal. Orwell? Kafka, I asked myself but the answer was 'No, East Berlin'.

From Berlin our production moved to Bielefeld, a small German town where it had been arranged we would perform our play to the officers and families of the British regiment stationed there as NATO forces. Our coach got there in the afternoon and we were housed by a cheery moustachioed officer in a section of the barracks of their contingents.

We performed the play to a good audience of officers, their American and German guests and their families, in an improvised theatre in what looked like an aircraft hangar. The play was well received and the colonel, or whatever rank the commanding officer held, proposed a vote of thanks when it ended. He invited the audience to a party that evening at the officers' mess, where they could mingle with the theatrical bouquet of talent from one of our great British universities.

We dressed for the evening and the contours of class began to emerge. A few of our men wore modest evening suits and jackets and the women wore demure evening dresses. The defiant amongst us were in black T-shirts and torn jeans, in leather jackets with metal studs worn without shirts and other gear which the officer class and their wives, our hosts, would not consider appropriate for a formal evening at the officers' mess.

The party began with the army families sitting around tables. There was a wooden dance floor and a German DJ had been called in for the evening. He played soft classics and sombre unobtrusive instrumental music and a few of the military couples danced foxtrots to Frank Sinatra and other soft shuffle numbers until some two or three of our boys and girls went up and had a word with him.

Yes, he told them, of course he loved hard rock himself, but he had been hired by these British soldiers and this was the sort of music they had ordered.

Ian told me later they had bullied the German boy into letting them choose the music and after the Stones' *Satisfaction* some even heavier rock came on. Most of our crew were on the dance floor now and moving in the unrestrained ways of free-fall dance.

Ian went back to the DJ. We seemed to have taken control of the party and he turned the volume up. The commandant's wife looked disconcerted and he was frowning. I could see that two of our administrative crew, very much public school lads who had probably been in their army or navy cadet corps and perhaps were even at University, noticed the senior officers watching our unruly crew and approached them.

I watched. Were they apologizing? Negotiating turning down the volume and instructing the DJ to revert to a more restrained or just softer choice of dance music?

Throughout the tour Michael and Celia, the two main organizers, had approached me deferentially and unnecessarily for every decision – shall we order breakfast at seven or seven-thirty? Should the props stay in the theatre overnight or would I approve of them asking the cast to carry the flats and furniture back to their bedrooms? But on this occasion, in deference to the commandant, they instinctively acted on their own. They approached the DJ and the music stopped abruptly. There was dismay on the dance floor and it turned to defiance.

'What the fuck's going on?' someone shouted.

A junior officer stepped into the silence.

'We don't expect such behaviour from Cambridge University students,' he said.

'For fuck's sake, we're only dancing, not fornicating in your precious mess,' Ian replied.

The commandant ushered his wife and daughters out. Michael and Celia rushed to apologize to our hosts.

'What the fuck are you sucking up to the fascists for?' one of the actors, with a distinct Liverpool working-class accent, shouted.

Michael's assistant tour manager was conciliatory but firm. We'd better get into the coach, the party was over. The dancers, perhaps twenty of them, turned to me. I shrugged. It was clear to me that in this circumstance, I had no authority. It was likely that Michael, Celia and the others who supported their good-mannered decision to defer to our military hosts thought I wouldn't understand the nuances that had caused offence and would, as an Indian, be out of my depth in this situation.

In fact, both Mala and I, having grown up in India as military brats in an ex-colonial army that slavishly imitated British tradition, appreciated very well the ways and prejudices of an officers' mess. Her brief glance conveyed exactly that to me. This was a fissure caused by the assumptions of class and both sides, Michael and Celia on the one hand, with the tacit understanding of Tristram, Felicity and even Bill Thomas, and Ian and the grammar school contingent on the other, would exempt Mala and me from taking sides.

My only concern was keeping what seemed to me to have resolved itself into one happy travelling family together. We headed north for Warsaw; though it didn't affect the performances in the least, there was a slight but distinct fall in the temperature of camaraderie on the tour.

When term began, Mike and I were summoned before our tutors. The commandant at Bielefeld had written a letter to the Master of Pembroke expressing shock and horror at the behaviour and language of our touring party. Mike had anticipated precisely such a letter and had solicited ten other from our hosts in the other cities where we performed, including a testimony of our good behaviour and talent from a senior officer at Gutersloh, the other NATO military station where we performed and where he testified that we had behaved in the exemplary way of the students of a great university.

The testimonials persuaded our tutors that the complaining commandant was at best out of touch with modern youth and mores and at worst, a bigot.

EZEKIEL

THE UNIVERSITY CAN be a small world; in my final year, a friend called Adi Katrak, a Parsi from Bombay who was on the same course and was a fervent disciple of Leavis, asked me if I wanted to attend the unofficial seminars of a brilliant critical mind, the possession of a man who was at the University but not of it.

I was intrigued, to say the least. This supposed genius was called Ezekiel and Adi said he had such authority that no one dared to call him Zeke or anything else. It would be like addressing Jesus as Jezza.

This Ezekiel was a mature student, perhaps thirty-five years old, who had written a thesis on D.H. Lawrence, which his tutors at the evening class rated highly and sent to a senior don at Cambridge, who invited Ezekiel to the University. The deal was that, considering his age and the fact that he had already graduated from the evening classes with some qualifications, he would be welcome to affiliate himself to the senior dons' college and write a PhD thesis on some aspect of working-class literature. The college, in recognition of his brilliance, would give him a scholarship and a grant to live on.

Ezekiel lived in a farmhouse on the outskirts of Cambridge with his wife Maeve and their eight children. This, Adi said by way of excuse, was because Maeve was a Catholic and didn't believe in contraception. They had married young and now their oldest children were teenagers who were enrolled in local Cambridge schools.

What Adi was inviting me to was, he said, fascinating seminars or lectures on neglected poets, novelists and essayists whom Ezekiel had researched and rediscovered. It was a cornucopia of literary output and could and would form an alternative canon. Keats and Conrad would have to look to their laurels when Ezekiel compiled and brought to the surface the hidden hoard of writing he was working on.

I went. There were about ten other undergraduates there and we all sat on the sparse furniture or the floor of the parlour of this old-fashioned farmhouse. We could hear the chatter of the children and the crying of the infants from the other rooms. Maeve brought pots of tea, carrying them with her free arm while feeding an infant at her breast with the other. She had long, dishevelled, unwashed, blonde hair and attempted unsuccessfully to hide her feeding breast under a tatty grey shawl which kept slipping off her shoulder as she dispensed tea.

Ezekiel had ginger hair and a ginger beard and lined cheeks above it. He was short and thin and wore a thick leather belt which held his cotton trousers quite high around his chest.

As I walked in with Adi and took my place without any introduction, I couldn't see his features as he was standing with his back to the window and the light silhouetted his form.

I didn't know what to expect. Ezekiel began his lecture by reading three poems he said he had discovered. They were by the same nineteenth-century working-class poet and described animals caught in and bloodily crushed by traps. His analysis of the poems, using notes he held in his hand but going off at tangents from them, was basically that concepts such as cruelty had grown from bourgeois notions and that there was, as the poet who was a trapper understood, no such squeamishness in nature. The growth of bourgeois sensitivity was designed to exploit at first the peasantry and now the working classes. He had, I deduced, a theory about the tyranny of concepts because he alluded to it. His audience must have heard it before.

The lecture lasted an hour and when he finished Ezekiel walked through the room and disappeared without a word to or from anyone. Maeve came in and offered the gathering tea and slices of home-baked bread. Adi introduced me to the others in the gathering with almost whispered names and nods. There was an atmosphere of deep thought and piety as we sipped our tea.

I asked if Ezekiel would join us and whether the audience was ever allowed to question him or disagree. One of the gathering – a tall, handsome, athletic-looking young man – said, in a hoarse whisper that Ezekiel found these lectures drained him of all his spiritual and intellectual energy and he had to go into isolation and meditate to recover. And no, there was no need to question him. Surely it was all crystal clear and self-evidently convincing?

When we left and cycled back to town and Adi asked me if I was impressed and would come again, I evasively said I'd think about it. I felt I had not so much picked up wisdom about an alternative canon of literature and method of criticism as wandered into the makings of a rather alarming cult. Apart from Adi, whose family I knew were Bombay millionaires, the rest of the apostles I met sported upper-class accents, undisguised by their hushed tones and respectful piety. I couldn't quite make out what Ezekiel wanted out of all of this. Adi hadn't told me that the apostles voluntarily collected sums of money and donated the pot to Maeve as Ezekiel wasn't to be insulted by any insinuation that he was receiving charity.

Mala told me on a weekend in Cambridge that we were going

out for a drink and dinner at a pub with Fi and her boyfriend. He turned out to be Philip, the tall apostle I had met at Ezekiel's lecture.

Over the evening I learned that he was reading theology, was a devout member of the Anglican Church and was the University's fencing champion. He was even being sent that summer to be tried for Britain's Olympic fencing team. I asked Fi if she had been to listen to Ezekiel and she said she hadn't been to his sessions, but that Philip had taken her over to the farmhouse and she got the feeling that he wanted Ezekiel to look her over and bless her with his approval. Behind this mischievous allegation, I could see there was some genuine conviction.

'What damned nonsense!' Philip said. 'He was curious about your being a Catholic since Maeve is.'

'Oh yeah, and did he want to know whether I'd have eight children and more to come?'

'Don't be silly, Fi,' Philip said.

'That's not silly. It's irreverent to the Prophet.'

'My dad was given a commission in the British Indian army,' I said, 'and when he wanted to get engaged he had to take his fiancée, my mum, to tea at the regimental colonel's house so that his wife could look her over and see if she was the sort of Indian they approved of as a regimental spouse.'

'That's what this was like,' said Fi, not wanting to give any ground.

'My mum determinedly wore a sari and no make-up and said she was a schoolteacher and the colonel's wife gave her a stamp of approval.'

'So did the prophet say I was okay?' Fi asked.

Philip was discernibly annoyed.

'I wish you'd stop being facetious,' he said. Fi leaned over and gave him a kiss on his cheek and in a husky voice said, 'Only teasing, darling, and yes, I want to go to the master's lectures. You have to take me. I am reading English after all and the hidden currents of literature call.'

In the coming weeks I didn't see Philip again, but whenever Mala was up with me, I would meet Fi. I soon learned that she had been to several of Ezekiel's lectures with Philip and had revised her opinion of his preaching. She could now see, she said, how coercive and cruel the class system of Britain had been through the prism of the writing that Ezekiel in miraculous ways had unearthed. It was a whole seething civilization which had been suppressed underground and Ezekiel was like the volcano, letting its energy and heat out into the world.

'Wow, pretty big claim, but Felicity, I heard three of the so called poems and they don't really compare with what we know of Keats or Yeats or even Ted Hughes, do they? He probably wrote them himself, you know.'

'You are steeped in class bias, and so is this University.'

Fi didn't need to acquire that class bias, she was born to it. She was tiny and freckled and her husky voice had first induced me to cast her in the chorus of *Murder*. Her speech and manners were patrician in the way of confident British girls. Despite the ideology she seemed to be absorbing from Ezekiel, she must have reproduced in some form the class prejudice of reading and criticism he railed against because she got a first in her finals and went home to her country house where she kept a pet pony.

◆

I didn't see Fi or Philip for two or more years after we all graduated and went our ways. I spent a year in Leicester and then returning with Mala, got a bedsit in Notting Hill. We'd both joined a radical immigrant political group of West Indians, Africans and Asians and as part of our routine commitment to meetings and agitation, we sold the group's newspaper in the evenings and on weekends in the immigrant areas of London and other cities.

Mala and I were assigned to Brixton, a South London area with a large West Indian population and a thriving market. We were distributing the group's newspaper and handing out leaflets calling people to a public meeting when Philip and Fi came up. We hugged and kissed. They said they had moved into a flat above the railway a few minutes away. They were married.

We went to their flat after our paper-selling stint and talked over the occasional rumble of passing trains outside their window. We caught up. Philip was working for a religious newspaper and Fi was in a publishing firm, determined, she said, to get to editorial level soon and find new and radical material to publish.

I asked after Ezekiel. He had gone to Devon with his family and was writing a novel, poems and a definitive critical work. And yes, they were still in touch with him and Maeve.

They had taken one of our leaflets for the political rally and asked if they could come. They did and we saw them regularly on the weekends when they weren't away in Devon with Ezekiel's family.

One Saturday, alone after my street and market duty as Mala was away, I rang the bell to their flat. After a while I heard footsteps on the stairs and Philip answered. He was dishevelled and looked as though he hadn't slept. He had dark circles under his eyes.

'You all right?' I asked.

'Come up ... I suppose,' he said.

He led me up and sat down on the sofa in their tiny sitting room and began to cry.

'What happened?' I asked, fearing the worst.

He shook his big head.

'No, she's not dead. Though I wish I was!'

I waited for more.

'They ran away. They must have been planning it for weeks because they hired a cottage somewhere and equipped it and they had even engaged divorce lawyers who sent me and his wife notices out of the blue.'

'How... when? What did you do?'

'The stupidest thing. I went to the house in Devon and Maeve and I and the eight kids cried together and then...' He stopped and sat down and held his head in his hands, 'then I slept with her.'

'Do you know where they are?'

He nodded and wiped his face with the end of his shirt.

'What are you going to do?'

'There's nothing to do, is there? She wrote me a note. I'll show it to you. It's cruel.'

'Don't show me,' I said.

'She said the notion I have of love is conventional and illusory and I beguiled her into believing in it and she thanks God that she has emerged from the hypnotic falsehood and found the real thing.'

'Come down and get drunk,' I suggested.

We did.

'I'm going to stay the night to see you don't do anything silly.'

Drunk though he was after several beers and half a bottle of brandy, he said, 'You have to stay, but don't worry, I'm not going to kill myself. I want to live long enough to expose that fraud and bastard. Do you know how much money I gave him over the years?'

'A lot, I expect.'

Philip left his flat and went back to the country to live with his parents.

Again, many years later I bumped into Celia and we talked

over old times. She said she had kept in touch with Fi. 'Ah Fi, she went off with that prophet of working-class love,' I said.

'Only for a bit,' Celia said. She told me that Ezekiel had moved on from Fi who was now in Malta in a nunnery and was serving her time in an apprenticeship and proving period in the hope of being admitted to the order.

VOICE IN A WILDERNESS

I SPENT MY last summer holidays doing what the University calls a fourth or holiday term. I had completed two years doing Natural Sciences and having taken the prelims and Part I of the Tripos, the Bachelor's degree qualification, I was obliged to spend another year at the University either doing a Part II in Natural Sciences, or doing any other course I chose, provided the tutors of that course would accept me, or indeed I could do nothing and just eat a requisite number of dinners in Hall and be deemed a Bachelor of the University when the year was over.

I had spent a great deal of time in my first two years hanging out with people who were reading English. They talked about books constantly and that led me to read every book that I considered would fill in the gaps of my very poor or narrow reading. I then proposed to my tutor, who had said perhaps I should study Economics or read for a Part II in History, that I'd like to read English and do the second part of my Tripos in English. He said that would be impossible as the course entailed learning Anglo-Saxon in Part I and knowing enough of a modern language such as French or German to translate some set poems from those languages. I'd then have to read Middle English, all of Milton and Shakespeare and do a paper on the modern, which I discovered meant nineteenth-century novel. I said all that sounded feasible.

Meredith, a zoologist himself, made enquiries from the English dons and came up with a solution. I could do English in my third year, which would count as the third leg of my Tripos by being exempt from the Anglo-Saxon and studying the history and evolution of the English language instead. I would have to stay in town in the summer holidays and attend three tutorials a week. I agreed.

I was assigned to my tutors and when the rest of the undergraduates went down for the summer break, I began my reading and writing in earnest.

What I had become aware of in my first year there was that all the copious reading I had done in India had been through an inspired haphazardness. As though I were a variation on Oscar Wilde's cynic, I knew the text of several works and the value of none of them. In Poona, I had in my early teens through school and college wandered into a decrepit building with a desolate Greek porch called the Albert Edward Institute. It consisted of three or four rooms full of books, most of them left over from the days of the Raj. The Institute by then, ten years after the captains and the kings of the Raj had departed, had very few members, most of them elderly men who would come to the veranda each day to read the stock of daily papers spread on trestle tables.

Very few people bothered to borrow books, which the membership of one rupee a month entitled one to do.

My friend and neighbour, Dara Cama, and I became members and read everything we could lay our hands on. I read every Thomas Hardy novel, even the obscure ones such as *Desperate Remedies* and *Two on a Tower*. I read the works of Marie Corelli and Bertrand Russell's *History of Western Philosophy*. We read the detective stories of Earl Stanley Gardner and P.G. Wodehouse.

I had no idea of how to evaluate what I was reading. There was no critical text on hand to guide this absorption. I couldn't have offered any criteria for Thomas Hardy's work being any better or worse than that of Marie Corelli.

At home in my grandfather's house where I grew up, there was one bookshelf in the sitting room. It had volumes of Kahlil Gibran's work, the autobiography of Mahatma Gandhi, the *Oxford Book of Modern Verse* and a large coffee table book titled *Parsi Lustre on Indian Soil* with photographs and life stories of the shopkeepers and other petty personnel who had paid to have themselves included. Again I had no way of evaluating or 'placing', as I learned to say at the University, the manifest humbug of Kahlil Gibran.

I had gone on to read all of Henry Miller and very many of D.H. Lawrence's books because they had the reputation of being sexy and outrageous, both of which my friends and I had ambitions to be. My Mamu, the one who was the disciple of Kammu Baba, introduced me to Jean Paul Sartre and to Albert Camus.

I remember my mother and her brother discussing *The Outsider (L'Etranger)* and *The Fall (La Chute*). My mother said she was puzzled by why these books were written as they were very depressing. I must have been fourteen and found her judgement intriguing. They discussed the plots. A man commits a random murder, he attends a funeral and another stands in a bar and for the entire book confesses his depravities to a listener. I wanted to read those books. My mother said they were not for me and so of course I got hold of them from my uncle's bedside and read them diligently.

I had very little idea that a discipline called criticism existed. I knew that films and books were reviewed in the papers and in magazines but it was only on being acquainted with the work of F.R. Leavis that I began to appreciate that there was a purpose and an artistic approach to the evaluation of works of art, especially those like poetry, prose and drama that used the medium of language.

Leavis was a cult at Cambridge in my time there and his work and contentions were bold, discriminatory and convincing. He founded the school of critical thought which started with the idea that literature was the central voice of civilization, that it had replaced religion as the arbiter of values, that it offered a culture the possibilities of thought and feeling, even the possibilities of life. If that was so, criticism had to be recognized as a primary discipline. It was the method by which the valuable would be separated from the trivial or ephemeral.

He was saying in all his works something very simple and I think I absorbed it. When a journalist asked me years later what was the one thing I learnt in Cambridge I said it was that one poem is better than another. Leavis evolved an approach to a work which assessed its sensibility. It was to literature what the Rosetta Stone was to Egyptian hieroglyphics.

I was taken by the sheer cheek of it and the universities were appalled and horrified by the same thing. Leavis and his works and articles had struggled for years to establish this system of discrimination. The undergraduates of the University, before my time and while I was there, delighted in the irreverence with which he treated texts and writers considered as gospel through the ages. They also looked forward to his attacks on living writers, on professors and panjandrums of literature.

His irreverence had earned him a degree of isolation from the University elite. He had been constantly denied a professorship at Cambridge by succeeding faculties who disagreed with him or envied his worldwide popularity.

I attended his crowded lectures in my last year and came away with what I thought at the time was a fresh critical vision or new perspectives on works such as *Hamlet*, the poems of T.S. Eliot or a D.H. Lawrence novel.

Ten years after Cambridge, I was earning my living as a schoolteacher in London and had been seconded by the Inner London Education Authority for a year to York University to write a thesis or paper on the teaching of immigrant children in British schools. I was pleasantly surprised to see in the York University bulletins that Leavis had been given a professorship by York and that he would be giving a series of lectures in that capacity. I went early to the first lecture thinking it would be as it had been in Cambridge, a pop concert crowd or one which would have done a football stadium proud.

I thought I'd come to the wrong college and wrong hall and went to check the venue. There were in the end three people apart from myself in the auditorium. Leavis arrived from York railway station in a taxi. He didn't seem deterred or disconcerted by the numbers. He read his lecture on Lawrence's *The Captain's Doll*, thanked us for our echoing applause in the empty theatre, collected his papers and left by taxi for the station.

I induced at least ten of my friends and acquaintances at York to attend the following lectures. Some of them, students of English asked, 'Who is Leavis?'

O tempora, O mores!

◆

In my final year at Cambridge, I received a letter from Able David, the editor of the *Poona Herald*, the small-town paper I used to report for as a student. He asked how I was getting on at Oxford, even though his letter had been sent, probably through him asking my aunts to post it, to Cambridge. He wanted a brief memoir of time at a British university. He had set down several questions to guide the editorial line my memoir should take.

I was amused by some of the questions: 'The food in Britain, is it good and are you missing home cooking?'

'Does everyone smoke a pipe and have you learned any bad habits?'

I didn't answer any of his questions but wrote a sort of personal article on the racist attitudes of some landlords and landladies and described the incident with the B&B in Gloucestershire. I wrote the article longhand – I had no typewriter and couldn't type even if I had – and posted it.

Two weeks later I got a note from Able saying he had not only published it proudly on the front page, but had sold it to the *Times of India* in Bombay and I would get a share of the fee that resulted. That was gratifying. His note also said that I should now turn my attention to answering some of the questions he had listed as he knew what would interest his readership. I never did answer his queries though I knew I was missing home cooking and had picked up very many bad habits even though I hadn't yet smoked a pipe.

Making friends with the undergads who were in my tutor group, we discussed what 'reading English' was all about. We talked about why we had chosen to do it. The influence of Leavis induced many of them (or us) to feel intellectually superior, with a sense of belonging to the elite, a Platonic philosopher-king caste.

At the beginning of my second year there was a scramble amongst the ambitious literati of the college to occupy the 'Crow's Nest', the room Ted Hughes used to occupy. It overlooked the croquet lawn and its window was obliquely facing the window of the room I had been assigned across the quad.

Marcus Grant, a Scottish colleague, won the toss and moved in. He was a gaunt young man with a thin face and searching eyes. He was going to be a writer. Indeed, he was one. He had already had two stories appearing in literary magazines published in London and in Australia.

I confessed to him that I too had ambitions in that direction and showed him three short stories I had written. He read them and said he was impressed and generously suggested that he would introduce me to his literary agent, Lawrence Pollinger.

I knew the name. Pollinger had been D.H. Lawrence's agent and Marcus never failed to mention this fact. He said I should write a letter introducing myself and he would write a note to the agency to recommend they take me on.

My stories were handwritten and the sheaf of three ran to forty pages. Marcus said it was only professional to send my potential agent typed copies. I had no typewriting skills but Enid came to the rescue. Her college had typewriters that students could use and she'd have them done in a day or two. She claimed to be a good typist and had worked as a secretary in the holidays.

I wrote as succinct and modest a description of myself as I could and sent the stories off in the post. I heard nothing for a month. Marcus persistently and politely asked me if I had received a reply. Eventually it came. The letter of rejection was nothing if it wasn't rude. It said my stories were unpublishable and bordering on unreadable. Lawrence Pollinger's judgement was that I should abandon the ambition to write prose and find gainful employment and that the agency never wanted to hear from me again. It was a 'don't-darken-my-day-or-doors-again' sort of rejection.

It was, I thought at the time, unnecessarily offensive. Marcus persisted in saying he liked the stories and thought them eminently publishable. Far from discouraging me from wanting to be a writer, it made me feel that the best retort – revenge would be too strong – would be to write some more and have a story or even a novel published and send it to Mr P. After all, I consoled myself, an agent, this one at any rate, was a commercial middleman with an unearned conceit. I told myself that if F.R. Leavis had rejected my writing I would be hurt.

A cutting of my article published in the *Times of India* was sent to me by post. On a weekend in London with Mala, she showed it to Adil Jussawalla. We were going for a drink in the local pub, The Denmark in South Kensington, a short distance from our bedsits. As we settled down to our half pints of bitters, Adil pulled the cutting of my article out of his pocket and was reading it when a wiry, obviously South Asian gentleman with a very noticeably hollow chest and abdomen, curly hair, thick eyebrows, and an imitation Lenin beard came and stood over the table. Mala and I wondered what he wanted till Adil looked up and recognized him.

He introduced the gentleman as Devapaksha, a Sri Lankan who was a writer and had a bedsit in the neighbouring building of his block. He had brought his pint of beer across, obviously hoping to join us and we invited him to.

'Deva writes very successful journalism,' Adil said, to break the ice.

The sunken Sri Lankan had, one couldn't help but notice, bulging round eyes like striker marbles. He accepted the compliment with a smile and a shake of the head.

'Farrukh here is a writer too,' Adil said. 'Look.' He gave Deva the cutting.

'How much did you get for this?' Deva asked, having barely looked at it.

'I don't know. Maybe fifty or sixty rupees?'

'Rupees!' Deva said with undisguised contempt. 'Why do you do this?'

I don't think any of us quite knew what he meant until he explained.

'You are spoiling the market going direct to these fucking editors in our countries. You are selling cheap. Bleed the bastards. They won't pay us brownies, but they will pay the white man, the sahibs. So use them. Hide behind the moribund bodies and masks of the white man!'

He was getting carried away.

'My editors have always been good to me,' I said. 'I mean I haven't written that much, just a few articles but...'

'Fuck "good to you",' Deva said and rolled his eyes. 'I keep telling Jussawallah that writing is not about arty and farty – it's about money. You are filtering the world through your mind for money. Don't you agree?' He looked down at the cutting to remind himself what my name was and added, 'You must agree, Dhondy!'

'I'll take as much money as I can get, but beggars and choosers and all that.'

'Have you branched out?'

'Branched how?'

Mala seemed quite amused by this conversation. The foam of her beer formed a moustache on her upper lip.

'Yes, lady, you can laugh, but I am trying to help your friend here,' Deva said.

'I'm not laughing at what you're saying. It's just I don't understand branching either.'

'I mean are you writing poems like Jussawallah or anything else?'

'I tried some short stories but they were rejected by an agent,' I said.

He turned his head as though to check who else was listening in.

'Fuck short stories and agents,' he said. 'Why don't you syndicate articles? This is very good. The whole world is curious about black men living in London. And black women. It will go on for a long time. Ever since the labour market has got internationalized, like Lenin predicted, this terrible curiosity is born.'

'What do you mean "syndicate"?' Adil asked.

Deva rolled his eyes again. Didn't we know anything?

'Syndicate is sending your article to a syndicating agency?'

'So it would seem,' I said. 'What's a syndicating agency?'

'Oh God. And you are an article writer?'

'Right now, I am still a student.'

'Yes, yes, I read this.'

Mala put her beer mug down and asked if we wanted another. She saw that Adil and I had got through our halves and Deva quickly downed what was left of his pint.

'Don't buy another drink here. Buy some bottles next door. You will get three times the quantity and you can come to my room and we can talk there. I want to introduce Dhondy to my syndicating agency but you must give them ideas. I will guide you,' he said.

'Good idea,' Adil said and I could see from his expression that he thought it would be strange or awkward but worth the trouble. Mala offered to get the beers. As we walked out Deva said, 'You see, you can get two pints in bottles for what these fellows charge in the pubs for one.'

'I thought you said we'd get three,' Mala said.

'I was exaggerating deliberately,' Deva said.

We went up the stairs to his tiny room on the fourth floor. Deva led the way. Adil indicated with his finger on his lips that we were in for a surprise.

The room had no furniture and there were old cushions without covers on the floor. There was no bed but against the wall and under the window that overlooked the street there was a wooden coffin. It was lined with a weary-looking quilt and there were blankets and a sheet at the foot of it.

'My humble abode. Sometimes jumble abode, sometimes tumble abode,' Deva said. 'Sit, sit, sit. Sit anywhere, I will get glasses and opener.'

He went out and came back with coffee mugs and a rusty penknife with a bottle opener attachment.

We sat on the scattered pillows and drank the tepid beer. Deva didn't seem to see the need to explain why he had no furniture or why he had a coffin for a bed. He very kindly began to give me advice on what articles I should write. Uncannily, his advice seemed in part to echo the questions that Able David of the *Poona Herald* had asked.

'Write something about how you have picked up British accents and habits. About food and about wiping your arse with toilet paper instead off washing like we do. And about bad habits like kissing in public.'

'What about an article on the different ways of teaching and learning that I have observed and absorbed – I mean from an Indian university where you learn facts to Cambridge which gets you to tackle problems.'

'Yes, you can write that, but don't be too disgraceful about India and praise your Cambridge. You see, what these British like black writers to do is to kick them in the balls, attack them for colonialism and racism. Some revisionist history, my friend, or the truth as we see it. Hah!'

He got to the point. I was to go with him to his agency; they would look at any articles I had to offer, and if the editor accepted them they would pay twenty times what I could expect from a single Indian paper; they would send the article to the hundred or more publications in the world which subscribed to their agency.

'Like Reuters?' Mala asked.

'More exclusive,' Deva said.

'But I haven't got any articles to show him,' I said.

'Get some,' he replied.

Adil lent me his beat-up typewriter and gave me some paper. I sat up most of the night in our basement bedsit and managed to write three 1,000-word articles. I was typing with one finger, soon two or three as I got used to the keyboard. The 'samples' were topics that appealed to me that night and not those that Deva had suggested. I was used to writing essays at the last minute for my tutorials. Deadlines had become a discipline.

At ten the next morning we went together to Lincoln's Inn Fields in Holborn. The agency was called Forum World Features and its editor was a young man called John Tusa. Deva had phoned him to say we were coming and we didn't have to wait. Tusa asked me about myself and wanted to see a sample of what I would submit. I warily handed over the three articles I had put together, noticing the typos and correcting them by overwriting in ink only after the page was painstakingly typed.

'I'd like you to wait outside while I read them,' he said.

I waited as asked. He called me in and said he liked them and said, 'Can you write regularly for us? I don't mean weekly but as and when you find something urgent to say?'

His secretary came in and handed him some papers from which he extracted a cheque for sixty pounds and handed it to me.

'I hope that's useful,' he said.

I'd never had a pay cheque for that amount. Work at the post office had been at the rate of twelve pounds for each week and walking dogs paid ten shillings an hour. I was stunned. I bought Devapaksha five drinks on the way back and he seemed happy at having done me the service. He was all smiles and rolling eyes and after two pints of beer and three whiskies, he fell over on the pavement and sat up grinning. I saw him home, helped him into his coffin, thanked him profusely and descended the four storeys to the street.

By the time I got to the room, it was late afternoon. Mala was still at work so I dozed my drunkenness off and told her the astounding news when she returned. We dined out at a Chinese restaurant that night.

In a week's time a large envelope arrived by post to the college. In it was the pack of syndicated articles on a headed and neatly cyclostyled copy. There may have been fifty or more pages in the pack of several dozen articles. I was gratified to see that one of my articles was on the front page. I didn't read the rest but skimmed through the first few. There was one on international affairs and there was a travelogue by a Chinese journalist who seemed to have gained access to war-torn Vietnam and reported on the poverty and despair in the places he, or it may have been a she, visited.

My other articles appeared in subsequent weeks again towards the top of the pack. I wrote several articles for Forum World Features in the coming months and lived off its largesse in a style which in my previous years at the University I hadn't enjoyed. Getting twenty pounds each time they accepted an article was a luxurious supplement to my scholarship.

It was when I finished at Cambridge and the subsidy of the scholarship ended and I went to London that the bonanza stopped. From London I began writing about things I had come across day to day. I wrote about the protests and demonstrations I had participated in against the Vietnam War. I sent in an article about the unfair arrests, which I witnessed, of black speakers at Hyde Park's Speakers' Corner. I wrote about the visit of Jyoti Basu, the leader of the Marxist Party of India, and his reception in London. Each of these articles was returned with a polite standard rejection slip. It was disheartening; I didn't know why the supposed talent, which had found generous acceptance, had suddenly and precipitately failed.

Mala gauged my mood after the third or fourth rejection and said I ought to stop sending FWF my articles and explore other syndicating agencies. I didn't. I was disheartened and began to look for casual work walking Chelsea ladies' dogs or washing up in kitchens.

Years later some facts came to light. John Tusa was appointed as the director of the BBC's World Service. An investigative article tracing his career noted that he had been the editor of Forum World Features. The investigation said that FWF had been paid for or subsidized in the main by an agency financed by the American CIA. It was implied that the syndicating agency was a front for American anti-communist propaganda. For strategic reasons and to maintain an appearance of balance or to throw foreign editors off the intention of the bulk of the articles, some leftish essays, preferably topping the pack, had to be commissioned.

It was an intriguing revelation and a somewhat wounding one as it characterized my articles as an ideological cover for CIA propaganda. I regretted not having read the packs in their entirety. Were some of the articles implying that Russian, Chinese or North Vietnamese citizens were cannibals who ate their children because of famines imposed by communism?

It wasn't at any rate a good start to earning one's living as a writer.

I sometimes wonder whether Devapaksha had any idea, whether he was in on the covert operation and, if he was, why was he sleeping in a bedsit in student land in a coffin?

THE MOVING FINGER WRITES

IN MY FINAL summer holidays, between my second and third years, my friends went off to distant places, to France and Greece and trekking in the Alps.

Meredith Dewey had proposed earlier that I join his bicycling expedition to Jerusalem. I wasn't tempted. It seemed like a long way to go. He said he'd done it before years earlier but this was a fresh adventure with a group of twenty who'd agreed to make the effort 'to make a pilgrimage to the Holy Land as Christians did in Medieval times'.

'But surely, they rode donkeys,' I said. 'Now there's a good idea. We can ride our bikes and you can hire a donkey. I happen to have the phone number of a donkey sanctuary near Ely.'

That was of course before we'd discussed what I would do with my third year and he'd ascertained that I would have to study through the holidays to catch up if I was to do my final exam in English. I was exempt from the bike or donkey ride. Dewey said the English department would fix me up with tutors over the summer and I would have to work hard and would only be allowed to sit for the English finals if my summer tutors found me capable.

Exemption from the expedition to Jerusalem was a relief.

One early morning, I cycled from our house to the college where the Jerusalem pilgrims, with packs and repair kits tied to their pillions, had gathered in the front quad. Meredith said he was sorry I wasn't going with them. They intended to cross Europe and the Bosphorus and cycle through Lebanon to Israel. They would return on flights but hadn't booked them as they didn't know how long they'd be. I waved them off.

I got down to work straight away, reading the plays of Shakespeare that I was unfamiliar with. In the next days I introduced myself to the three tutors to whom I was assigned.

My Middle English and Chaucer tutor was called Catherine. She was a large lady, in her late fifties with long blonde but usually unkempt hair bunched and tied with a flamboyant ribbon near the end. She lived on King Street which was famous for its six pubs and the undergraduate tradition of a challenge which required the victim to drink a pint or two in succession in each and see if he could stand up unaided at the end of the street.

Catherine's house was one of what appeared to be an authentic Elizabethan terrace whose walls were brick and white plaster between transverse wooden beams. The walls looked like they were leaning dangerously and the stone floor, though carpeted, gave the impression of being uneven and sloping towards one wall. The front door, heavily curtained, which opened directly on to the very narrow pavement of King Street, had a crooked jamb and lintel.

The house was small, cosy and warm with its old sofas crammed into the front room, and felt as though it was about to collapse. It had a large curved glass window looking out on to King Street and Catherine displayed perhaps ten book covers, placed on the sill for passers-by to look at and wonder.

Catherine assured me during my introductory visit – I was looking perhaps apprehensively at the beams which held up the ceiling – that I was safe.

'Yes, I know it looks like it'll come down any minute, but it's been going for four hundred years and the town's surveyors have done their tests on the whole row and pronounced it sound and stable.'

She was curious about my background and why I wanted to switch from sciences to English. She said she wanted to start straight away and asked me what I'd read of Chaucer and when I told her I'd attempted to read *The Canterbury Tales* and the poems, she picked up a volume from her shelves and read a few pages aloud, in rhythms, cadences and an accent that made the meaning plain.

Her tutorials were a delight. She put complicated ideas very simply. For her no poetry was obscure. It was all in the music. After we came to the end of the second tutorial, she proposed we go to the pub where she'd buy me a drink and we could discuss the essay I had written. She was known at all the pubs and confessed that she had been around them for maybe twenty years.

In the second week of this extra term I received something of a shock. The foundation which paid my scholarship wrote to me saying that the college had communicated to them the fact that I was having extra tutorials during the holidays and the fees for these had not been anticipated in the estimated cost of my scholarship. They weren't saying they wouldn't pay, but they had to consider the addition to the sum allocated to me and that would take a few weeks as the London office had to refer to the Foundation office in Bombay.

I didn't know how to react to this. I dashed off letters to my parents and one to Mrs Vesugarh who I was sure would determine whether the scholarship paid the extra or not. I tried to explain why I had switched courses, assuring her that my science qualification was safe and I would be awarded a BA on the strength of it. I also said the Foundation could consider the extra money for these tutorials as a loan which I would repay as soon as I began to earn some money.

Meanwhile, I continued with the tutorials. I said nothing to my two other tutors, but I confided in Catherine.

'Until I get a reply from the Board in Bombay, I'll stop coming to you,' I said, 'and I'll come back if they agree to the fee.'

'You can't do that,' she said. 'I don't want any fees from you. I enjoy our sessions and interaction and I shall let your college know that I don't want to be paid.'

I was about to protest when she added, 'But it's not charity. I want something in exchange.'

I was intrigued. What could Catherine want from me?

'You're a Hindu,' she said.

'I'm not, I'm a Parsi, a Zoroastrian,' I said.

'But you're Indian and grew up there,' she said.

I didn't know what she was getting at.

'Do you know anything about the theory of karma?' she asked.

'Not technically, but of course living in India one picks up most stories and beliefs of Hinduism.'

'I want you to tell me, as a sort of exchange, everything about the theory of karma. I don't want to read about it, I want it from you,' she said.

I was inclined to say I didn't believe in any religious philosophies, but here she was waiving her tutorial fees in exchange for anything I could tell her.

'Is that a deal?' she asked.

I said it was and we got down to discussing the *Wife of Bath's Tale*.

I went to the University library that afternoon and found the shelves on Hindu philosophy. I went to the library again the next day and the next and putting aside my English studies took copious notes on the Upanishads, on the Buddhist theory of the cycle of births, on reincarnation and how one's deeds determined the form one would assume in later lives.

Karma appeared to me to be a pernicious doctrine. It seemed to say that people who were born blind were deprived of sight because they had done something to offend against the act of seeing in their previous life. All suffering was caused by transgressions in previous existences.

And what the hell was I doing? I, who considered myself a Marxist or at least some form of socialist who had turned away from the opiate of the masses? A feeling of absurdity crept over me, but I had to do it. Besides, I wondered why Catherine wanted to know any of this. But I knew I was not to question why. I had to teach myself and explain as best I could to her.

I did, and we talked about the tenets that guided good action and separated it from the bad. I had to admit that the teaching on ethics and the life that would lead to reward in the next was a bit unclear. In the great epic, the Mahabharata, Krishna who is God incarnate, tells Arjun, the hero of the epic, that killing is not per se wrong, that he can slaughter his cousins in a war if that is his 'dharma', the duty to which he was born as ordained by his previous karma. It's only the Buddha and the teachers of the Jain faith who put down strict ethical rules against killing, against unkindness, against deceit, envy, theft, etc.

'Ten commandments?' Catherine asked.

'Probably more than eleven,' I said.

'And not caring about another's pain would count as one of those?'

'I don't suppose any human can care about the pain of everyone.

I am sure there are starving children in India but every Hindu can't be held responsible for their suffering,' I said.

'But suppose one caused their suffering?'

'A black mark in your karma register, I suppose.'

'And can one ever atone for that? In Christianity, in my Catholic faith, repentance leads to forgiveness. Does the idea of repentance, being sincerely sorry for the wrong you have done, alter the record, erase the black mark?'

I could see that she was disturbed by her question, anxious for the right answer.

'I don't think the theory of karma allows repentance. What's done is done.'

She turned her head away and when she turned back I could see her eyes were filled with tears.

'Shit!' she said.

'Did I say something wrong?' I asked.

'No, but tell me, how does one get rid of bad karma or can't you ever?'

'I suppose you accept the punishment of being reborn as a lesser creature, take your punishment and try and be good in the next life. But Catherine, isn't it all nonsense?'

'I don't know. Isn't Catholicism all nonsense then?'

'Well, it's easier. Stick to it and truly repent for whatever it is you've done.'

'Whatever it is,' she repeated slowly.

'I think there is a prescription that devotion and ritual can sort out the bad karma. I'll check that out.'

'Farrukh, I don't think anything will sort me out,' she said and went into the kitchen and fetched two glasses and a bottle of brandy. She poured us both a general peg and settled down on the sofa and seemed to be inviting me to do the same.

'Let me tell you why I'm bothering you with all this,' she said.

◆

As a young Don she had fallen in love with a professor. She said she wouldn't tell me his name. That he was an expert on Milton was all she would say. He had returned her affection and they had had a whirlwind affair despite the fact that he was married, had three children and lived a seemingly happy life with his family.

She said she was very much in love with him and they went away for a month to India together. He told his wife he was on a lecture tour of the subcontinent and that she would have to see the children through their school term while he was away.

They had an idyllic time in India but when they returned the horror struck. On the day of their return, the professor's wife killed herself. She threw herself under a bus in town. She had left the children with her parents for the weekend. She left a note saying she knew all about their affair, had found the letters Catherine had written and deduced what her husband had written in return. She didn't think she could live without him and his love or live with the lies, the shame and the scandal.

The professor took a year's leave of absence and took his children away from Cambridge. He ended his affair with Catherine, who discovered that she was pregnant and when she, by letter, refused his demand that she abort the child, he cut off all contact with her.

She gave birth to a boy, Jonathan, whom I had met when he dropped in during one of our tutorials. He had graduated a few years earlier from Oxford and now worked in London. He had never been told who his father was or that he had stepbrothers and a stepsister and she was dreading his finding out. He would, at the least, ask her why she had brought him up in ignorance of his origins.

She felt most for the completely oblivious and innocent woman she knew she had selfishly wronged.

I downed my brandy in one shot. She poured me some more and the tears now streamed down her face.

'Do you go to church and to confession?' I asked.

She shook her head.

'Lapsed when all this happened.'

'It was a long time ago.'

'Thirty years,' she said.

'I think Catholicism and confession are the better bet,' I said.

'Tell me, is there punishment in this life in the theory of karma?'

'I think there can be,' I said. 'There are stories in Indian mythology which prove that in the end one has to drink from the chalice one poisons.'

She nodded, dried her eyes and proposed we finish the session in the pub.

She didn't mention her sorrow or demand any more of karma from me. We moved on from Chaucer to Scottish ballads and then to the history and evolution of the English language. The holidays came to an end and I threw myself into a term of serious work with 'lit. crit' essays on books one had to read in a hurry.

A few weeks into the term a man I didn't place at first knocked at the door of our house.

'Got the right house. I checked with your college. Farrukh. How are you?'

It was on hearing his voice that I recognized Catherine's son Jonathan.

'Jonathan, come in! What's up? I know I've neglected your mum. I should go and see her...'

I saw the gaunt expression on his face and stopped.

'So you haven't heard! Mum died a couple of days ago.'

I was stunned. He seemed to be taking it sombrely but calmly.

'Oh, we knew about it for over a year. The cancer was spreading and it got to her brain as the doctors said it would. It was a matter of time, that's all, and time caught up.'

'I didn't know,' I said.

'She left a note for you, that's why I'm here. I think she wants you to say something at her funeral. It must be in the note. At least that's what she said to me.'

He said he had to go and told me where and when the funeral would take place and that he was staying in her house for the time.

The note was addressed to 'Farrukh, my karmic friend.' It asked me if I would kindly consent to read the extract from the Bhagavad Gita which I once read to her about life being an illusion caused by consciousness and then whether I could follow it up with twenty specific lines from the *Wife of Bath's Tale*. As a post-script she wrote: 'And I did take your advice and tried the old repentance–forgiveness trick when the padre came to see me in the hospital.'

I did the readings she wanted and wondered if the mourners who had gathered understood what I was reading or why.

A PROPOSAL

IT WAS TIME, we thought, that Mala stopped being Mrs John Snow, which is what her passport labelled her. Johnny went with her to a friendly and cheap lawyer in London who told them that they would merely have to sign an affidavit to say that their marriage had never been consummated. A judge or magistrate would be presented with the affidavit with neither or one or both of them in court and he or she would pass a judgement annulling their union. They would be single individuals again.

Would that mean she would have to surrender her British citizenship, since she obtained it through being married to a British citizen? No. She could remain British and even apply for a passport in her maiden name. And so it was done.

Years later I discovered that an obscure provision of British colonial law specified that the children of a person born in Burma when it was still a British colony could claim British citizenship. Mala's grandfather had been a Bengali judge posted in Burma by the Indian colonial justice department and her grandmother was an Englishwoman he had met and married in Calcutta. Her father was consequently born in Burma and she could have claimed UK citizenship without the rigmarole we had contrived. Ironic afterthoughts!

Though she had kept it a secret for years, Mala told me that one weekend after the annulment had gone through and I was busy rehearsing a play for the Pembroke Players, Johnny had come down to London and landed up at her bedsit. He said he wanted to stay the night and it became clear to her that he was in some sort of nervous state. She made him a bed on the floor of the tiny bedsit and when she decided she wanted to turn in, she asked him to switch the light off.

As she got into the single bed, she could see his silhouette sitting up in the dark. The darkness must have given him confidence because he began to speak.

'I didn't marry you to help you get a passport, you know. I fell in love with you that first time I saw you in Bombay. He had already told me that you and he had sort of drifted apart and that made me feel I could try and get close to you but I was absolutely gutted when it became clear that he and you were very absorbed with each other. I went through with the whole thing and averted my eyes and shut my ears. It's been torture, Mala, and I know it's stupid, but I hated going to that lawyer and getting our thing annulled. Your passport with my name in it was the distant candle in that blight. I still love you and always have since we met and I know you don't know that so I came down to tell you. I had to tell you.'

He was quiet after that, sitting with his legs drawn up to his chest in the dark.

'I wish you hadn't told me,' she said. Her heart was beating faster and there was a lump in her throat. How could she have not noticed even a hint of the passion his voice so deeply expressed?

'Is that all you're going to say?'

'No. No. I just didn't know or suspect and now I feel stupid and sort of blind. God, am I that insensitive?'

'Maybe, or maybe I'm a damn good actor, better than your

fucking Pembroke Player, my best friend and sensitive, perceptive human being who didn't catch on either about my feelings throughout all that.'

He paused.

'Or maybe he did and even does now and doesn't give a shit as long as he's got what he wants – you!'

'I think you're being unfair,' Mala said. She sat up in her bed.

'Well, if he knew then he too is a damn good actor because he didn't give even a hint. You won't tell him I came down and about all this, will you?'

'No,' she said. 'But I'll tell you something. I've kept all her letters and I can show you. My mum wrote to me saying that you – she called you "that British boy" – "wouldn't have done all this just to help your sly Parsi boyfriend. He must be deeply in love with you to do all this and one day it will come out and God knows what might happen. Baby, I have known these secret love triangles to end in tragedy. In my days in Lahore I knew a young man who was secretly in love with his sister-in-law and finally he stabbed his brother to get her and he was caught and hanged."'

'Good story,' Johnny said.

'Please! It's a horrible story and I thought it was stupid her telling me it, but now you say she was right.'

Johnny didn't reply for a minute.

'Don't worry. I'm not going to kill your precious Parsi and get hanged.'

'What are you going to do?'

'I'm not making you nervous, am I?' Johnny asked.

'Of course not. Confused, but not nervous with you. We are friends, aren't we?'

'I want to be more than friends,' he said and when she didn't reply he added, 'I want to make love to you,' and he stood up and went to the bed and held her and tried to kiss her.

Mala said she turned her head. He wasn't forcing her; it was a gentle attempt or overture and when he saw it wouldn't succeed, he withdrew, put on his shirt and shoes and coat in the dark, took his overnight bag and without a word walked out of the door, shutting it silently behind him and out of the house and into the night.

When Mala related this to me, she said he never alluded to any of it ever again.

EXIT

AFTER OUR FINAL exams and the interval before the results were published, we were called to the convocation to receive our degrees. We lined up on King's Parade in the order we had for our individual college matriculation ceremonies, wearing hired gowns and caps, to be awarded our degrees by passing in line through the Senate House, kneeling before the vice chancellor, being awarded the scroll and walking out into the sunlight with the realization that Cambridge was not home any more. The rooms, houses, hostels had to be vacated that day. One didn't belong any more though the conceit that you were taking something of the spirit of the town with you would embed itself in most of the graduands, however absurd that is.

On graduation I received a letter from the Atomic Energy Commission of India. It congratulated me on my Natural Sciences degree and offered me an interview with a view to offering me a job at the Commission in order 'to serve your country'.

The world and I were aware that India and specifically the Atomic Energy Commission, despite all its years of propaganda and Nehruvian statements about 'Atoms for Peace', was, under the prime ministership of Indira Gandhi, developing a nuclear bomb.

It was the only prospect of a return to India and employment that had come my way.

My parents were in Iran. My father had resigned from the army and after several years as the town engineer of a company steel town, had taken up a contract to work as an engineer on a steel plant that the Shah of Iran was developing in Isphahan. I had no ancestral home to which to return. There was my father's family house, built by my grandfather and proudly named Dhondy Terrace in the alleys of once-rich Byculla, a central area of Bombay, which was now occupied by my father's younger brother; as army itinerants we had no claim on the property though I would always be welcome to use it as a base.

The truth is, though, that I didn't want to work as a junior scientist, a cog in the machinery that would provide India with a nuclear weapon. I had read accounts of the life of J. Robert Oppenheimer, a socialist who felt compelled to race to make the atom bomb for America and was devastated when he saw the genocide it inflicted on Hiroshima and Nagasaki. I was, with all the arrogance and unearned intellectual certainty that possessed me at that age, politically and morally against nuclear bombs. And yet, apart from walking dogs for the ladies of Chelsea or vacuum-cleaning their houses for an hourly rate that would buy a meal, I had no prospects of a job. Graduating meant the scholarship was over.

There were other reasons I couldn't go back to India. The least of these was that Mala and I had no money to buy flights back and having eloped we wanted to live together, even if the living was confined, as it was, to basement and attic bedsitters with single gas rings to cook on and bathrooms shared with other tenants of four-storey Victorian terrace houses of Kensington and Notting Hill.

In India, the search for employment, most probably in a university, the social conventions, the pressure of families would not allow us this crammed but exhilarating romantic freedom.

So we stayed in London and discovered another world – in which the only landlords who would rent you a room if you were black or Asian were Asians or immigrants themselves; in which pubs wouldn't throw you out, but would leave you standing as though invisible, at the bar; in which hooligans would take to 'Paki-bashing' for fun; in which advertised jobs, excepting the most menial, would have been filled by the time you made a phone call and told them your name.

Political activity at Cambridge had revolved around discussion, argument and bussing up to London with others to join protest demonstrations. In London the necessity for politics to be more than talk became evident. We – the bedsitter crowd of friends, including the poet and writer Adil Jussawalla, the writer and archivist Ratnakar Kini, the painters Praful Dave and Tarun Bedi, Dolly Thakore, Mala's friends Brinda 'Bini' Das and her sister Radha – would go to Hyde Park corner to listen to radical speakers. We would join the protests against the Vietnam War and in favour of immigrant rights.

Beginning as ideas, convictions and arguments in India and at Cambridge, the political commitments and tasks gradually permeated all our days and weeks. Yes, occasionally we called each other 'comrade', but with a tongue slightly twisted into one or other cheek.

SUNLIGHT ON THE GARDEN

THE MAY BALLS famously take place in June. Several of the colleges, but not all, plan to hold these events with featured rock bands, flowing champagne and the college halls and garden marquees erected in the quadrangles for the late night rave. The tickets are prohibitively expensive but still it was obligatory to attend at least one May Ball in the three years you were there. It's a formal ball and the dress code is black tie and evening gowns. Of course saris and Indian sherwanis or closed-collar Nehru jackets are allowed.

The expense is regarded as the last extravagance of the year, so undergrads save or borrow to meet it. One for the memory!

In our last year, my close friends and I decided to go to our various college balls and then meet up at 2 a.m. when the different college festivities are thrown open to the revellers from other college balls. It's a free-for-all, or at least free for those who've paid to go to one.

Eight couples pledged themselves to the plan. We'd finish with the balls, get into four punts which we'd reserved and pole our way downriver to the village of Grantchester, have a drink on the riverbank, punt back to Cambridge and make our way to the house that Mathai and I shared to have breakfast, the ingredients for which we had bought and set out in our kitchen on the day before.

Everyone in this group and almost everyone else I knew who was graduating that year had a firm or at least fair idea of what they were going on to. Most of them had, through the University Careers' Advice service, had interviews and got appointed to a step on the career ladder they hoped to climb.

My interviews at the Careers' Advice offices to which my tutor insisted I went were frustrating. I couldn't turn up and say I wanted to be a writer.

The adviser to whom I was assigned had a file on me and began by noting that I had a two-part degree.

'Natural Sciences and then English,' he said. 'Not unknown, but unusual! So which direction would you wish to pursue, unless you want to combine the two and write about science for some publication.'

'I could do that,' I said.

'I thought you might say that and rang up a few people. The only thing in that field that was going was subediting a technical medical journal. Getting the correct Latin spelling for guts and balls and tits, you know.'

'Doesn't quite sound my thing,' I said.

'You are more Physics, aren't you? Well, there's a job in the laboratory of a boot polish factory just outside London,' he said.

He saw from my expression that I didn't want to make a career of that.

'Then how about publishing? There aren't any job interviews I can send you to, but some factual or scientific publishing houses or departments will, I am sure, be willing to speak to a well-qualified young man about prospects in the field.'

He said he'd send me possible appointments for exploratory talks and names and addresses through college. He never did.

Of course I was at the time writing the occasional article for Forum World Features but that was hardly a career. The thought had crossed my mind to ask FWF if I could work part-time in some editorial capacity there. After all, they accepted everything I had written for them so they must trust my judgement.

The other option, as Mala had generously offered, was that I could stay in the bedsit and write and we would live modestly off what she earned until I finished and sold short stories or articles or even a novel. It seemed the only option with the addition that I could undertake menial odd jobs for a part of the day and write for the rest of it.

Mala had surprised me by spotting on the noticeboards outside her local newsagents a typewritten card offering to sell a second-hand typewriter for a couple of pounds and had tracked it down and bought it.

'The fellow who sold it to me said he was a writer and had written several novels on it so it would bring my writer boyfriend good luck.'

'What was his name?' I asked. 'Someone famous?'

'He told me but I was so excited at the thought of finally getting hold of a typewriter that would be yours that I forgot. It'll come back to me though.'

It didn't come back and that left me often thinking as I worked on it who could have been the prolific novelist-owner. And if he lived in a rooming house in Earls Court then his several published novels hadn't enabled him to buy or rent his own flat! So it wasn't Angus Wilson or Kingsley Amis.

Mala and I danced the night away at Pembroke. None of our gang had opted for my college's May Ball but we knew very many fellow graduates. We waited for the chimes of 2 a.m., and then fled to King's down the road. They were all there and we ball-hopped and hall-bopped and drank champagne till we were happy or silly and then all sixteen of us proceeded to the hired punts.

Things went to plan. As we passed under the bridges over the Cam we had to watch out for the maniacs who followed the tradition of stealing bicycles and throwing them into the river from a high bridge for the devilment of hearing the splash. They'd be dredged out by the police or council workers in subsequent weeks to be sold at auction to the next batch of undergraduates.

It was dawn and there were young men and women in various varieties of formal dress and even in various stages of undress, sitting in groups or lying on the Backs, the grassy verges banking the river. Our itinerary entailed changing punts to get from the lower to the higher river across a lock and changing back on the way to our house and breakfast. We had carried buckets of ice with champagne which we fetched from a college room as we made our way to the river and having popped them all we were as merry as intended.

As we passed under the bridge at Trinity College, a tall young man, wearing a hat and raincoat over his day clothes with one camera hanging round his neck and another poised against his face to take pictures, leaned over the parapet and snapped furiously as our punts crossed under the bridge. The boys in one of the punts had taken off their jackets and shirts and were poling the punt bare-chested. In one of the punts, Ariel, Dickie's Swedish girlfriend, an adventurous and uninhibited young woman with whom he occasionally spent the night in our spare room, waved at the photographer who now ran down off the bridge and along the banks of the river following our punts and snapping away.

'What are you doing?' Ariel asked him as he persisted.

'Taking pictures.'

'It'll cost you.'

'Really? You'll have to catch me first!'

'Why are you taking pictures? There is nothing to see?' Ariel asked.

'I think there is,' the young man said.

'Oi, are you an artist photographer?' Ariel asked.

'I try my best,' the lanky young man with platinum blonde curly hair said. He was still walking along, changing cameras, adjusting the focus and snapping away at the punts and the people with a studious intensity.

'Do you know *Dejeuner Sur L'herbe*? The painting?' Ariel asked.

'Yep,' he said.

'I'll give you one better,' Ariel said and she stood up in the punt, undid the button at the back of her dress, wriggled her shoulders out of it and let it drop to her feet.

We all clapped. She then undid her bra, stepped out of her dress and now wearing only her knickers lay down in the punt and turned her torso towards the photographer.

He was obviously animated and clicked away. The passing punts and people on the banks cheered. Ariel stretched out her hand to the photographer.

'Give me your hat, make it interesting,' she said. The young man threw the hat into the punt and she put it on and posed in a parody of the woman in Manet's painting, sitting up with her knee drawn up and her hand on her chin. Dickie and Ian behind her also struck a pose. Mathai, who was poling their punt, took a rest, allowing the punt to drift slowly. The photographer couldn't believe his luck.

'Thank you, that's great, that's perfect!'

'Now I give you your hat back if you send me a copy for my grandchildren,' Ariel said.

'I'll be happy to send you five. Tomorrow. Where shall I send them?'

'Get in the boat, we'll give you some addresses,' I said.

He stepped from the banks into the punt I was poling and we steadied it.

'You want a hand with that?' he asked.

I handed the pole over to him.

He was quite expert at it and straightened the punt out and streamed away in a few poles.

'So what are you taking pictures for? You are not at Uni are you?'

'Good God no, I've come down from London and been snapping all night.'

'You must be wiped out? Do you want to join us for breakfast?' Mala asked.

'Sure, that's very kind of you.'

The young man squatted down and stretched his arm out.

'Andrew Whittuck,' he said, introducing himself.

Mala shook his hand and told him our names and said, 'The Manet lady is Ariel. She's going to make you famous.'

'So what are these photographs for?' I asked.

'My editor at the agency thinks she can sell a feature called Cambridge Madness to all sorts of magazines, here and in Europe. Only problem is I haven't found the right writer,' he said.

'You just have,' Mala said.

We discussed the feature over breakfast. I told him how I might tackle the subject and he seemed excited.

When would I be in London?

As soon as I was required.

Would I be interested in some other jobs that he had lined up for which we could go fifty-fifty?

Like what jobs?

'Well, for one, there's this pop group which hasn't yet put out a single but they're about to and we can see if it gets in the charts. They are not very well known but they've agreed to be photographed and my editors say they can sell an article on a new band at the start of their possible career. They are playing in a basement in Tottenham Court Road. We can go down and listen and maybe talk to them there and fix proper times for later.'

'Sounds great, what are they called?'

'Don't know what it means, but that's pop bands for you. They call themselves Pink Floyd.'

A FAN LETTER

January 2016

Dear Clive James,

I've been reading your latest poetry collection and your essays on the last books, essays and writers you've read. You've made no secret of your illness or its terminal nature, but the essays and the poems, though evocative and somehow universal, have never-say-die or go-gentle balls about them. Enough. Look forward to even more reading.

I don't think you'll remember me, but we went up to Pembroke the same year as undergraduates – you as a mature student, I as a scholarship-wallah from India.

Several of our contemporaries at Cambridge went on to become famous in one way or another. There were playwrights, there was your fellow Australian, Germaine Greer, who made her name as a feminist and an academic, there were actors and even a politician or two who made their mark, but I've chosen to write to you because you were out of the ordinary.

You must remember the first weeks of that first year when I looked forward to sitting somewhere in your vicinity at Hall with a crowd of undergraduates, the two Americans Sandy Mack and

Stephen Greenblatt, both of whom went on to become academics in America, and a fellow called John Hay.

None of us knew each other but somehow, as non-British undergrads, we had come together.

You had no inhibitions about launching into anything that interested you. You talked with the conviction that your audience would be compelled to listen.

You regaled us with stories, anecdotes and a remarkable familiarity with popular and high culture which I thought was unique. You seemed to be able to speak about almost anything. If someone asked how long it took a caterpillar to crawl from Cairo to the Cape, you would probably have a plausible answer.

I could see in those first days that this ability was envied and resented by some of that gathering at dinner at the long tables where stupid public school boys threw buns at each other. You had the air of being busy, constantly engaged with more important matters altogether elsewhere. You wouldn't stay after dinner but hurried away and left the others to discuss what you had said.

You may recall that you were organizing a reading of Poetry of the Thirties' and you came and knocked at my door to ask if I would read the work of Day Lewis. I was flattered but didn't realize that you had chosen me because you thought my Indian accent was closer to Day Lewis's Welsh and it would perhaps amuse the audience. I only became aware of this reason for your choice when Berry remarked that my speaking rhythm echoed the Welsh. It went some way to my determination never to change the accent I had grown up with.

A year later I was inducted into the editorship of the University poetry magazine called *Carcanet*. I was told, and I think I told you, that the magazine had been first published in the late nineteenth century as a joint venture between Oxford and Cambridge with contributory poems from both. It had been dormant for several decades and had been revived for one trial before I inherited the editorship. The revival of the magazine entailed getting a professor of English to be its patron and I decided to approach Professor L.C. Knights at Queen's and ask him if he would oblige.

I had asked my friend and later housemate, Mathai Joseph, a postgraduate student researching computer techniques, to be the 'manager' and look after the accounts and practicalities. The two of us knocked, very nervously, at Professor Knights' door one evening and presented our request. He was very kind and said of course he would back such a venture and that he looked forward to the next issue. He offered £30 from some professorial literature fund towards the publication.

For the second issue I worked on, I asked you for some poems. The next day, at dinner, you promptly handed me a sheaf of perhaps fifteen poems. I had advertised the brief for *Carcanet* and was going through several submissions from poets and aspiring poets.

Reading the poems I was convinced that twelve of them stood clearly in technique and preoccupation above the efforts of the other submissions we were considering and in consultation with my co-editor in Oxford decided to devote perhaps half the issue to your work, without declaring it a 'Clive James issue'.

I got a friend to ask the sculptor Elizabeth Frink if we could use a photograph of one of her works as the cover. She agreed and we did.

When the issue came out we sold out the edition. The reaction from the aspiring poets of Cambridge was, though not unexpected, entertainingly vehement. A coterie of poets at King's who ran a magazine called *PAWN*, not professionally printed as *Carcanet* was, but run off on a cyclostyling machine, was vehement in its denunciation. The poems were worthless as literature – they were at best amusing showbiz verse... I had to face this stuff down and decided to laugh it off rather than provide literary critical criteria for having chosen it.

You were aware of the criticism but contemptuous of it. You sat next to me at dinner the evening of the publication and said we should go for a beer afterwards.

Over that beer you said one thing that I have remembered all these years.

'If you learn nothing else from Cambridge,' you said, 'you should learn that one poem is better than another!'

We were never close enough or personally involved to regard each other as friends and only met at these poetry occasions, except for the one time you directed my inadequate acting talents in a sketch at the Footlights. I can't remember what the plot or point of it was but the main character was played by Germaine Greer, who recalled us doing it when we met decades later at a literary festival in Kerala at which we were both speakers.

Talking of which, you went to India some years ago and wrote a novel arising from your sojourn. I must admit I wrote a rude but truthful review of it for, I think, the *Sunday Times*. I won't make an excuse for that but will venture to ask you what you would have made of a 'novel' if I had written one about Australian life after a week's holiday in Alice Springs?

I have indeed followed your career in TV and read your essays and poetic works. Your translation of *The Divine Comedy* is the best and most accessible that I have come across and as a fan I can say I buy your poetry collections as they are published.

Let me end by saying I haven't forgotten how in my first days at Cambridge you were kind to me. In the company of the undergraduate dining companions one evening, I joined in the conversation and, perhaps after a beer or two, in telling some story of how I'd got into a fight in London, said 'was kicked in the groins'. John Hay promptly quipped, 'Where do you keep the other one?' The company laughed.

I immediately realized that my Indian-oriented English usage had confused the plural of 'loins' with the singular of 'groin'. You didn't laugh. You asked how the episode concluded and feigned interest. When we walked down after dinner, out of hearing of the rest, you said, 'Don't bother about them, sport!' or words to that effect.

I had recovered from my embarrassment.

'Groins? Indians have two, you know. Double the capacity, double the fun!' I said.

You grinned with a crooked mouth.

Ever

(Though as Auden wrote when he modified the last line of his famous poem from 'We must love each other or die' to 'We must love each other and die.')

signed,
Farrukh Dhondy